CURSED MATE

SHADOW CITY: ROYAL VAMPIRE

JEN L. GREY

CHAPTER ONE

I clutched the phone as I waited for the line to ring. I shouldn't have been holding it because Tennessee was a hands-free state, but I didn't care. Annie needed to answer my call, and I felt more in control holding my phone to my ear.

After ringing once, her phone sent me to voicemail. The automated voice informed me, yet again, that the mailbox was full. Like I hadn't already known that. I and Eliza, Annie's and my foster mother, were the ones who'd filled the damn thing up.

Foster mom was no longer strictly correct. Annie had turned eighteen, and I was edging closer to twenty. Eliza didn't have to take care of us any longer, but she chose to. She was our mother in every sense of the word, and I wasn't sure what would've happened to me if she hadn't taken me in the morning after my fourteenth birthday. Annie and I had discussed this same thing three days ago on her birthday before she'd left to meet up with her boyfriend in Shadow Terrace.

Her flipping boyfriend.

The problem.

Something was wrong. I could feel it in my bones.

I'd heard how he had talked to her. He was a sweet talker and a damn manipulator. Messing with her mind and threatening that he wasn't sure what would happen if she didn't come back to see him soon. Suggesting that maybe he'd take solace with someone else. The kicker was she fell for it every single time, which surprised me. Prior to meeting him, Annie had been the strongest person I'd ever known.

I huffed and tossed the phone onto the black cloth passenger seat of my cherry red Mazda 3. I'd bought this car several months ago back home in Lexington, Kentucky which was a blessing. Otherwise, the five-hour trip south down the interstate and through Nashville and Chattanooga would've been a lot more challenging. But Shadow Terrace wasn't much farther away.

Annie always answered her phone. I'd teased her mercilessly that it had become an extra appendage, one she never went anywhere without. But she'd been acting strange ever since she'd run away to visit Shadow Ridge University against Eliza's wishes, two months earlier in April, and right before the application deadline. The university was in a neighboring town to Shadow Terrace.

She'd never done anything like that before, and Eliza had felt hurt and betrayed. We never would've found out about her visit if it hadn't been for Annie's boyfriend, who called constantly, demanding she return to the university.

When Eliza had asked why she'd gone to Shadow Ridge University, Annie had explained that it was a very exclusive place and she felt like she was meant to go there. Eliza had told her that slum lords attended the college, but Annie wouldn't be deterred.

After returning, Annie had lost interest in every other school, which right there had been a red flag. She'd turned down every acceptance letter to the Ivy League universities without any hesitation.

I had a feeling her newfound singlemindedness was due to the asshole who'd talked her into running down to Shadow Terrace again this weekend.

Annie and I used to hang out on weekends, watching television and planning our lives, but this weekend, she hadn't even called into her job at the children's shelter to tell them she wasn't working. We hadn't caught wind of her sneaking away until they'd called Eliza to see where she was. She'd worked at the shelter since she was fifteen, saving up to gain the best college education.

This guy not only had her acting strange but flaking on a job she claimed gave her life purpose. If I hadn't known her so well, I'd have thought she was a druggie needing her fix, but I'd heard lust could make someone act that way too.

Not that I'd know.

The sun dropped behind the mountain range, changing the pretty pinks, purples, and oranges in the sky to the cool, dark shades of twilight. Normally, I'd have pulled over to take in the beauty, but not today. It was just another reminder that Annie hadn't called us in two days or returned this Sunday afternoon. So here I was, heading down to Shadow Terrace to check up on her.

My foot pressed harder on the gas pedal, increasing my speed to well over eighty. I shouldn't have been going this fast, but with every passing second, I felt more hopeless.

Calm down, Ronnie, I scolded myself. I couldn't let my imagination get carried away. Maybe her phone had died, and she'd gotten stranded on the road.

Okay, that scenario wasn't much better. Annie always

gave me shit for thinking the worst, but there had to be a plausible explanation for her silence.

My GPS told me to take the interstate toward Georgia, and I passed through the lit-up downtown area of Chattanooga. The GPS said Shadow Terrace was about forty minutes from here. I only hoped that those minutes went by faster than the last four and a half hours had.

My phone rang on the seat beside me, and I nearly swerved off the road to grab it. It was about damn time Annie called me back. Anger replaced my fear as I hit the green button, not bothering to look at the name. "Took you long enough."

"It's me." Eliza sighed. "I take it you still haven't heard from her."

"Of course not," I bit out and immediately felt bad. I softened my voice. "I'm sorry. I just mean I would've called you if I had."

"No need to apologize." Eliza chuckled, but the sound fell flat. "I was hoping you'd forgotten to call me and that everything was okay. I hate that I didn't go down there with you. If something were to happen to either of you—"

"Stop." I refused to let her consider the possibility. She'd already lost so much. Her family had died in a car wreck like the one that had claimed my parents. That was one reason she'd wanted to foster me—she could relate to the pain of how I'd lost my mother. Now Annie and I were the only family she had. "I'll find her." I had to. There was no other choice.

"Just make sure nothing happens to you." She *tsk*ed. "You've already given up so much for her, holding off on your own future to help set her up for college and pay the bills."

Eliza had been bringing this up more and more often—

the fact that Annie was going to college in a few short months, whereas I'd barely graduated high school a couple of years ago and spent all my time working long shifts at an Italian restaurant to help Annie save money to go. Eliza kept telling me I was avoiding my future and had become too focused on helping everyone else but myself. Maybe I was. Part of me still wasn't at peace, and I didn't understand why. It was like I didn't belong anywhere, but I liked living with Eliza and doing whatever I could to help Annie succeed. They were the only two people who had been there for me my entire life. I'd do anything for them.

"Nothing will happen to either of us, and I told my manager I needed a few days off. Everything is fine." Okay, I couldn't promise that, but I needed to hear the words too. Maybe if I said them convincingly enough, it would make them true.

A girl could hope.

"I'm a horrible guardian." Her voice grew tight. "I ... I shouldn't have let you leave without me. It might not be safe."

"You have to work early in the morning." Her bladder was the size of a pea. We'd be stopping every thirty minutes. The trip would go by much faster with her back home. "Besides, I can take care of myself."

"Maybe, but there is so much going on in this world. If something happens—"

"I'll call you." I wouldn't pull the same shit Annie was. "I promise. And I'll let you know when I find her."

"Okay, just be safe." She hung up the phone.

That was a pet peeve of mine with her. She never said goodbye. When she was done talking, she ended the call. It didn't matter if I was done talking or not. Rather than call her back and scold her, I bit my tongue. She was pushing sixty and had taken us in out of the kindness of her heart. She deserved respect. Hell, she'd earned it.

I pulled off I-24 and followed my GPS onto a twisting two-lane back road.

Maybe I'd plugged in the wrong address. Annie had made Shadow Terrace sound like a quaint but happening town, but I wouldn't have been surprised if cow pastures started popping up. Nothing but trees surrounded me, and no cars drove the opposite way.

The moon slid behind clouds, further darkening the road. I turned on my high beams and leaned forward, like that might make a difference.

A chill ran down my spine, and goosebumps spread across my skin. Under normal circumstances, I wouldn't have paid any mind to that, but my gut was telling me to turn around *now*, sensing danger. But that was insane.

Paranoia hit me hard, and my heart rate increased. I was alone in my car, and there was nothing threatening nearby, but my pulse jumped so hard I felt it beating in my pressure points.

I inhaled sharply, trying to clear my mind, but something *yanked* inside my chest.

Stop it. I had to use my head. *There is nothing wrong.* Great, I was losing my mind. Pretty soon, I'd be having complete conversations with myself.

A sign appeared next to a long wooden bridge ahead, and I slowed the car.

WELCOME TO SHADOW TERRACE

Thank God. I wasn't lost after all.

Determined to find Annie, I pushed my irrational fears aside and proceeded across the bridge. I hadn't let my imagination go wild like that in a long time. When I was younger, I'd see a dark shadow flickering in my room, especially at night. I'd scream and cry to the point that no foster parent could take it. I'd bounced from house to house until, on the night of my fourteenth birthday, a shadow approached me in a group home I'd been staying in. My screaming didn't stop until morning when the warden decided to take me to Eliza. Instead of growing frustrated with me, she would hold me every night, keeping the demons at bay.

For the first time in my life, I'd felt safe. All because of her. That was why I had to find Annie and bring her home. Eliza needed us.

About a mile past the sign, the trees thinned, and a cute town appeared. The Tennessee River ran beyond the town, just like Annie had described. The closest buildings were white with red roofs and varied in size. In the center of town was an enormous gray stone building with a dome on top. It stood out from the other buildings but at the same time ... didn't. Obviously, the businesses and the central building had been designed in the same era, but the one in the center felt different from the rest.

It was the landmark Annie had described as sitting right across from the bar where she and her boyfriend would hang out every night during her visits.

And that was exactly where I was going. It was my only lead to finding her. Even if she wasn't currently inside, someone should be able to direct me to her.

As I bumped over cobblestone roads, I saw couples strolling on the sidewalks, hand in hand, looking smitten with each other. I drove down the road, which was lit up with old-fashioned gaslights, and searched for the bar Annie had described. Strangely, there were no stop signs or traffic lights, but mine was the only car in sight.

Two figures wearing dark hoodies over their heads stepped out from a building shadowed in darkness. Not an inch of skin was visible, despite it being summer and hot as hell, even at night. What kind of idiot walked around dressed like the Grim Reaper? The only thing missing was the scythe.

I'd seen some runners trying to sweat, but these two were walking slowly. Maybe they were part of a secret society—that was the only thing I could think of—but from what I'd seen in movies, secret society members didn't wear their outfits in public.

Whatever. I wasn't staying in town long, so it didn't matter. To each their own.

As I approached the domed building, I noticed a three-story white building directly across the street with a sign labeled Thirsty's Bar.

It was the only bar in sight, meaning this was the place Annie had mentioned.

I rolled my eyes. Whoever'd named the place must have thought they were being clever.

This town was so odd.

I couldn't wait to get the hell out of here.

Back home, it was hard to find a metered spot downtown, but here, the parking spots were open for miles. I parked in front of the bar and climbed out of the car. A warm breeze hit me, but the earlier chill returned. It reminded me of the chill I'd feel when I was younger before the shadow would appear. I grimaced and chided myself for being dramatic. Five years had passed since I'd imagined a shadow coming after me, so my unease had to be from the unsettling situation I'd found myself in.

That was all.

I wrapped my arms around my waist and hurried across the street as the smell of honeysuckle wafted around me, putting me more on edge. I couldn't shake the feeling of being watched and wanted to get inside.

Once. I'd look behind me once, and that was it. The door was only a few feet ahead anyway.

I glanced over my shoulder ... and stiffened.

A man five inches taller than me and with dark eyes stood two feet behind me. His irises were ... outlined in crimson? I blinked, thinking I was seeing things; then a sickly ripe-apple cinnamon scent attacked my nose. The back of my throat dried, either from fear or the overwhelming stench.

"Hello, there," he cooed with a slight Irish accent. "Are you lost?" He tilted his head, and the moonlight reflected off his short ebony hair. His skin was fairer than mine, which said a lot, considering my natural red hair and pale complexion.

Stranger danger blared in my mind. "Nope. Not at all." My legs stopped moving, and I was practically frozen in my tracks. Neither fight nor flight instincts were kicking in.

Figures. I'd turned into an icicle instead.

"Are you sure?" One dark eyebrow arched, and his gaze landed on my neck.

Odd. Normally, guys stared at my boobs first. Any other time, I'd have been comforted by that, but it just upped this guy's creep factor. "Yup, I'm positive. Just looking for a friend."

"Friend?" He leaned closer. "I've never seen you here before, so I'm thinking you're lost."

He was really hung up on me being lost. "I just got here."

He stared at me like I was a tasty meal. I took a step backward, and the corners of his mouth tipped upward.

"Let me help you find them." He touched the ends of

my long copper hair. "A pretty girl like you shouldn't be walking the streets alone at night."

My breathing turned shallow, and my back pressed against the wall next to the entrance. "I'm good. She's inside." I prayed she was. I wanted to find her and get out of here.

"Well, I'm going in too." He brushed past me and opened the door, waving me in as he said, "Ladies first."

A breath I hadn't realized I'd been holding left me, and I practically ran through the door, wanting to be around other people.

When I stepped into the room, it was as dark as the night outside. My eyes tried to focus as the man grabbed me by the waist and pulled me into a corner. His head lowered to my neck as a scream built inside me.

CHAPTER TWO

His mouth was so close to my neck I could feel his cool breath. This guy was a psycho, and I needed to do something.

I placed my hands on his chest to push him away, but his weight vanished, and I stumbled forward.

"What the hell is going on here?" a husky voice with a slight accent I'd never heard before asked. It wasn't quite English, but there was something alluring about it.

I managed to catch my balance and not fall flat on my face. I glanced up at my savior ... and my world tilted.

Soft blue eyes scanned me as the man's face lined with worry. Unlike the asshole he had clutched around the neck, this man's skin was fair but slightly more sun-kissed than mine. He was a couple of inches taller than my attacker, putting him at around six feet. Even though his athletic body was tense, he had a regal posture emphasized by a white button-down shirt and black suit.

He was drop-dead gorgeous, and that *yank* made me take a step toward him.

"Are you okay?" the man asked as he examined my neck.

Did I have something there? That was the second time within five minutes someone had focused on it. Absently, I placed my hand at the base where the loser had tried to lick me.

At least, I hoped it was licking.

Wait. Ew. Maybe not.

But that would be better than being bitten, right? I could wash off saliva, and we wouldn't be intermingling bodily fluids. My stomach revolted. *Shut it, Ronnie. Focus.*

"Uh ... I am now." *Oh, dear God, shoot me.* He was going to think I was hitting on him. "Since you helped get the weirdo off me." I tore my gaze off Sexy and glared at the creeper.

Sexy snarled at the guy and pulled him closer, getting in his face. "What do you have to say to Miss..." He paused and glanced at me expectantly.

I gawked at his hard chest. I bet it would feel nice to touch...

"Are you not going to tell me your name?" Sexy asked, a hint of humor lacing his voice.

The longer I stayed quiet, the worse this whole situation would become. "Ronnie." I winced. I sounded like a little girl, and I didn't want him to think of me that way. Yeah, right. I knew why. "I mean, Veronica, but my friends call me Ronnie."

His eyes twinkled with mirth before hardening as he looked back at Creeper. "What do you have to say to Miss Veronica, Klyn?"

My name sounded way too good rolling off his tongue. I could listen to him say it repeatedly and never grow tired of it.

Ugh. *Lock it down, Ronnie.*

"Klyn," Sexy warned.

Klyn wasn't much better than Creeper, so it fit.

"I'm..." Klyn trailed off as his nose wrinkled. "I can't do this. She's just a—"

In a blur, Sexy slammed the asshole into the wall beside me. He placed his forearm on Klyn's neck and lowered his head to stare into his eyes. "If you want to make it out of here alive, you will apologize."

"Prin—" Klyn started, but Sexy pushed harder on his neck, and the guy's words cut off with a groan.

We had to be causing a scene. I looked around the dark-ened room, which my eyes were acclimating to. Several couples were sitting at the bar, all in various states of passionate kissing. One guy actually had his hand on the girl's breast.

Gawdy, red velvet booths lined the perimeter of the room where a few groups of couples were sitting together. Even then, they were either ogling their partners or had their hands in inappropriate places. One guy had his mouth on a girl's neck while she writhed underneath him like she was on some kind of high. She had to be getting one hell of a hickey.

What was this place, and why was Annie hanging out here?

My hand clamped on my neck. They'd have to pry it off me while I was in here.

The craziest part was that no one was paying attention to the commotion we were causing. Eliza had been right that this wasn't a safe place. Everyone was on drugs or something—even the bartender didn't turn in our direction.

"I'll release my hold on you, but if you say anything

other than 'I'm sorry,' I will kill you," Sexy growled, his jaw twitching. "Do you understand?"

Wow. That was intense. But this entire place could be described that way.

Maybe this was one of those happy-ending places.

Klyn nodded, and Sexy loosened his grip.

"I'm..." Klyn said as he frowned, keeping his focus on Sexy, "s-sorry."

"Are you saying that to me?" Sexy smirked and placed his free hand on his chest. "Well, thank you. But now I want you to direct it to her." He lifted a brow, daring the asshole to defy him.

"But she's—"

"Do not make me angrier," Sexy warned, and shoved Klyn so hard that his head hit the crimson wall.

I didn't understand why Creeper wasn't fighting back. He clearly didn't want to apologize to me, but he wasn't fighting. He was taking the punishment.

"Fine." Klyn rubbed the back of his head as his tongue ran across his teeth. He turned to me and sneered. "I'm sorry, Miss Veronica." The words were mocking, but he had muttered them, even against his will.

That had been the entire point. Sexy expected obedience, and this was his way of putting the guy in his place. But Klyn still had a predatory gleam in his eye.

Predator.

That was the perfect way to describe him.

"If you mess with her again, there will be problems. You know better than to cross me." Sexy let go of Klyn but didn't move from where he stood. He rubbed his hands together and glared. "This is your one warning. Do you understand?"

"Yeah, I got it," Klyn spat. "Can I go now?"

"Go get me a drink." Sexy nodded to the bar. "I'll be there in a minute."

Klyn cut his eyes at me then stalked off.

No matter what he said, I could tell whatever had happened between us wasn't over.

"Are you okay?" Sexy asked me. "I'm so sorry about that."

"It's not your fault." I forced myself to laugh, hoping to diffuse the situation, but it came out more like a croak. "It's not like you're his king." Though he did look like royalty, which might be why I'd said something so random.

He started as a genuine smile spread across his face like I wasn't privy to the joke. "I am not his king. You're right about that."

"See." His smile stole my breath, but I powered through it. No one had ever affected me this way. This had to be how Annie felt with Douchebag—meaning I had to leave.

Immediately.

"Well, thank you," I said. I saluted him and walked past him toward the bar.

A cool, strong hand grabbed my arm. "Where are you going?"

Okay, maybe he wasn't such a nice guy after all. The type of guy who made you feel safe only to destroy the illusion was the worst type of asshole. This seemed more in line with Annie's man and made Sexy's attractiveness not quite as tempting.

"Excuse me," I bit out, wanting him to know what he was doing wasn't cool. Removing my arm from his hand, I cocked one hip and placed a hand on it. "I don't care if you helped me. Do *not* touch me like that again."

He stepped in front of me, blocking my way.

"Then don't make me." He straightened his shoulders, adding an inch to his height.

I wished I was taller, coming in at five foot five, especially when dealing with pompous jerks like this. Even if I stood on my tiptoes, I'd just reach the top of his shoulders. "How would I *make* you?"

"You walk over there by Klyn again, and he won't be able to help himself." His face went slack, and he cleared his throat. "Then I'll have to get involved again, and things will escalate. A girl like you shouldn't be in a place like this."

"A girl like me?" I wasn't sure whether he was complimenting or insulting me.

He bit his bottom lip, a bit of insecurity bleeding through. It was charming. Dammit. "Yeah. The kind who isn't desperate for attention."

He was right. I wasn't that type. In fact, I hated being the center of attention. "Well, I'm not looking for that."

"Really?" He crossed his arms. "Then why are you here?"

I didn't want to tell him. I was getting mixed vibes from him. One second, he came off like a good guy, and the next, I questioned his motives. But he had saved me from the neck licker, and I'd come here to find Annie or someone who knew her. This was the safest option ... or maybe the dumbest. "I'm here looking for my sister."

His eyes narrowed. "Why don't you call her?"

Anger bubbled inside me. "Oh ... man." I smacked my forehead. "You're right. Why didn't I think of that?"

"Sometimes even I forget about these things." He pulled out his phone and gave it a peculiar look. "It's kind of too convenient."

Grasping sarcasm was not his strong suit. Or he was

making fun of me. Either way, I was over this strange encounter. "I tried doing that, dumbass."

"Oh, well, maybe she's in her hotel room." He waved a hand. "I don't see any single ladies here."

"Are you quoting Beyoncé?" This guy was hot but odd.

"What's a Beyoncé?" He looked over his shoulder. "Is that your sister's name?"

"No, it's—" I stopped. I was wasting time when Annie could be somewhere in this bar, getting groped. "You know what? It doesn't matter. Her name is Annie, and she's not in her room because she came here to visit her boyfriend."

"Wait ..." He lifted a finger as his face turned into a mask of indifference. "You're saying your sister, who doesn't live here, has a boyfriend who does?"

"Yes." He had to be slow. All men this sexy had a major flaw. Stupidity had to be his. "You see, people can date each other even if they don't live in the same location. It's called a long-distance relationship. You might not understand that since you probably have women lined up to get in your bed." I nearly growled at the thought. What the hell was wrong with me? I was usually good at keeping my mouth shut, something I'd learned quickly growing up in foster homes. But the longer I stayed here with him, the looser my tongue got. And the worst part was ... I wanted to be one of those women.

Nope. I needed to cross my legs the entire time I was here.

He winked. "You might be right about that, but I will say a woman has never captured my attention like you."

Yep, player. That confirmed it. But my stomach still fluttered. "Uh ... thanks." I forced my attention away from my sporadic heartbeat and focused on my best friend. "But seriously, have you seen her? She has long dark brown hair, bright brown eyes, and a kind smile. She laughs a lot—she's the type who lights up a room just by walking in."

Eliza had made me feel safe, but Annie had warmed my ice-cold heart. Despite being orphaned, she'd had better luck in the system and had come to Eliza as a baby. She radiated kindness and worked her ass off to make a better life for herself and help others wherever she could. That was why I didn't mind giving up my own education to help her pursue hers; I knew she would change the world for the better—something I'd never do. My goals were to help Annie succeed and take care of Eliza.

"Wait." The corners of his mouth tilted downward. "Is this your sister or your lover?"

"Touché." I laughed unexpectedly. The combination of the question and his disappointed face caught me off guard. "No, she's my sister and my best friend. Remember, she's here visiting her boyfriend."

"I'll tell you this." He placed a hand on the small of my back and led me toward the door. "I've been here since six, and no one here has matched that description the entire time."

"That's not reassuring." I'd hoped to march into the bar, grab her by the ear, and yank her outside. That was how things happened in movies when someone was acting childish, so it made sense for me to treat her that way. "Okay, do you have any suggestions on where she could be?"

"You know what?" He opened the door. "I bet she's on her way home like you should be."

The wind blew past us, and I damn near drooled at the scent of syrup. Hmm ... maybe there was a breakfast restaurant around here. Breakfast was Annie's favorite meal, especially when she had a few drinks in her. I sniffed and followed my nose.

"Uh ... do I stink?" Sexy mashed his lips together as if he were trying not to smile, but mirth wafted off him.

Why would he—oh, I was sniffing his chest. That wasn't breakfast food but him. What kind of guy wore cologne that smelled like syrup? I could breathe him in all night, not to mention nibble—*Rein it in, Ronnie.* "Sorry, I thought I smelled breakfast. I didn't mean to sniff you."

"If you want to eat breakfast off me, we can arrange that," he said huskily as he brushed my cheek. "I'd be a willing participant."

The thought of him naked flashed in my mind, and my face blazed. I had to get my head on straight. "No, that's not what I meant, but ... thanks." My voice rose at the end as if asking a question.

The humor vanished from his face, and his body tensed. "You need to go. Now."

"What?" His change in demeanor gave me whiplash. "Fine, but do you have any idea where I might find my sister?" I had to remember I'd come here for Annie, not to waste time talking to a man.

"Alex," a woman said from behind us, her voice sultry. "What are you doing out here with her?"

So that was why he'd gotten upset. He must have known that his date was approaching.

Two could play that game. I was going to make him feel uncomfortable. After all, I hadn't done anything wrong.

CHAPTER THREE

A small part of me was hurt. This guy had helped me and flirted with me, but he was now giving me the cold shoulder because his girlfriend had arrived.

What a freaking pig.

I stepped aside to see the woman, and for a second, I wondered if I batted for both teams.

Her chestnut brown eyes inspected me from head to toe as her cranberry lips pursed. She ran four-inch burgundy nails through her sexily tousled, shoulder-length ivory hair, making her black crop top inch up and showcasing flawless alabaster skin. She leaned back against the brick wall and crossed her ankles, causing her black miniskirt to rise, and I wasn't sure how her vagina wasn't showing.

In other words, she was gorgeous, and envy coursed through me, which was absurd. I'd just met this guy, and I didn't have any claim on him. "Oh, he was just offering me the opportunity to eat breakfast off his body."

"Are you serious?" Her eyes turned to slits as she stared Alex down.

"Oh, Gwen." Alex smiled boyishly and draped his arm

around my shoulders. "Don't worry. I only made the offer to her, not other nonresidents here."

My God, he was shameless. He seemed encouraged by our reactions. He was incorrigible. Now that he wasn't even denying it, I was the one who felt uncomfortable. That was my usual luck. Sometimes, I felt cursed.

"He was teasing."

"Now isn't the time for shit like that." Gwen glared, not hiding her displeasure. "You're old enough to know better."

"Yes, Mom." Alex chuckled as he pulled me closer to his side. "But since I'm already in trouble, I might as well make it worthwhile." He waggled his eyebrows.

This town was freaking insane. What kind of guy blatantly flaunted another girl in front of their significant other? Hell, her hair was probably messy because they'd had a go at each other already.

Something hard settled on my stomach, and I acknowledged it. I was jealous for no reason whatsoever. After tonight, I'd never see him again, which was best for everyone.

"Not funny," Gwen said curtly. "I will make your life a living hell tonight if you don't behave."

"I've got to go anyway." I was now even more desperate to find Annie if these were the kind of lunatics she was hanging around. I should've pushed her to let me come with her instead of staying behind. Then, maybe things wouldn't have gotten so far.

Alex dropped his arm from my shoulders, and I frowned when I realized I missed his touch. Instead of being too warm to the point that I felt suffocated, something I'd experienced with everyone else I'd dated, *his* touch felt cool and refreshing, even through the material of my shirt.

Even though I'd never had a boyfriend, I had dated, but

each guy had gotten so damn clingy that I'd felt trapped, and their touches had made my stomach churn. Before Annie and Eliza, everyone I'd trusted had hurt me. It was easier to keep people at arm's length and enjoy the freedom of doing what I wanted when I wanted. That didn't go over well with guys when they got more serious about me than I was about them.

Alex nodded, his smile vanishing. "Now *that* is a brilliant idea." His expression turned icy. "You should leave this very instant." He motioned for Gwen to head into the bar. "I'll be right there. Let me make sure she gets out of here."

"Gladly." She humphed. "But if you don't hurry, I'll come back and handle this problem myself."

Wow. I hadn't done a damn thing to justify her threatening behavior, but the way this night was going, I wasn't surprised.

She spun on her black stilettos and sashayed into the bar, conveying a confidence I'd love to possess.

As soon as she entered the building, leaving the two of us alone, Alex took my arm and dragged me toward my car.

"Wait." I tried to stop, but his grasp was strong as he hauled me to the vehicle. "How do you even know that's my car?"

"You said you came to town looking for your friend." He paused and smirked at me mockingly as he gestured around us. "And there's only one vehicle here that has"—his eyes flicked to my license plate—"tags from a different state."

Yeah, that had been a stupid question, and his answer proved he wasn't as slow as I'd thought, making him even sexier. *Ugh.* I had to stop obsessing over his looks and wonderful smell. So what? I'd seen sexy men before. It wasn't like he was the only one I'd crossed paths with.

Well, he was the hottest, but there had been others *half* as attractive as him.

He stalked to the car, and I had to jog to prevent him from ripping my arm off. His hands were strong yet soft and smooth. It was a perfect combination, one I'd never experienced before, equivalent to peanut butter and chocolate.

"Damn, can you give me a second?" Obviously, he was desperate to get to his girl, but I wanted to keep my arm attached. "If you're in that big of a hurry, just go back inside."

"I would if Klyn wasn't keeping tabs on you," he hissed and winced. "The last thing I need is him coming out here and accosting you while I'm preoccupied with Gwen."

Gwen. Damn. Now I hated her even more for absolutely no good reason. "Preoccupied of the breakfast variety?" The words slipped past my lips, and I hoped he hadn't heard them.

A low, raspy chuckle emanated from his chest as he spun toward me and leaned against the driver's side door. The red complemented him, and the moonlight made him even more drool worthy. The light brought out the golden highlights sprinkled throughout his hair, revealing that it wasn't as dark as it had appeared indoors. "Why? Are you jealous, Veronica?"

My full name rolled off his tongue as if he had been destined to say it. He made it sound like a risqué love song.

"No!" I exclaimed a little too loudly. "It's just, you mentioned—" I inhaled sharply, forcing myself to shut the hell up.

It was for my own good.

His nose wrinkled with disgust.

Great, I might as well throw myself at him. I'd known him for less than ten minutes, and I was getting all clingy. If

I'd been in his position, I'd have been thinking the same thing. I needed to cut my losses and split.

I pulled my keys from my back pocket and let them dangle. "Okay, you're right. I need to go."

"Yes, you do." He didn't move, and after a moment, he lifted a hand. "Why aren't you going?"

"Wow." He was making fun of me. This night kept getting better and better. "You think you're hilarious, don't you?"

He tilted his head and bobbed it side to side. "I like to think I have a good sense of humor, but I'm lost as to why you're asking. If I tell you that I do, I might need to reconsider my assumptions about myself."

This conversation had gotten unexpectedly philosophical. "No, I mean, you're standing in front of my door. How am I supposed to leave if you don't move?"

"Oh, right." He grimaced and moved a few steps away from the door. "Forgive me."

Yeah, I wasn't responding to that. I unlocked the car door, and he brushed my hand as he opened the door for me.

My skin buzzed from his touch, and I had to restrain myself from touching him more.

"Uh ... thanks?" He might have been doing it because he was desperate for me to go, but I didn't want to be a complete asshole. He had helped me, after all.

He leaned closer, his deliciously sweet smell surrounding me, and whispered, "You're welcome."

My mind fogged, but I cleared my throat, hoping it would help me think straight. I slipped inside the car, needing to put distance between us.

As I started the car, he stood in the open doorway, staring at me.

"Take a picture. It'll last longer." The cheesy saying popped out.

He waggled his brows. "I didn't think you'd be up for that, but I'm down if you are. Maybe I could cover you all over with breakfast instead."

Heat fueled my body, and I licked my lips. "No, that's not what I meant."

"I know." He brushed his fingertips across my arm. "Go home so you'll be safe." He shut the door and walked across the road, not bothering to look both ways.

My body hummed with an indescribable emotion. A strange part of me felt as if he were walking away with a piece of my soul—which was absurd.

At the door to the bar, he stopped and turned back to me. I had to be crazy because, when his gaze locked with mine, I could swear it was full of longing and regret. His chest expanded as he waved and mouthed *goodbye*.

Right. I had to leave. I tore my focus off him and pulled the car onto the road. I hated to admit that it took every ounce of self-control not to look in the rearview mirror. Alex expected me to leave, and I planned to—once I found Annie.

I drove deeper into town. The buildings were clustered more closely together, and the road led toward the river's edge. The sidewalks were bare, except for one couple walking hand in hand. What was it with this city? Strange people and couples everywhere. I'd barely seen anyone alone, just Klyn and Alex—who seemed to be with Gwen— and no one in groups.

A few blocks down the road, I found a white building slightly larger than the rest with a sign stating it was the Shadow Terrace Inn.

I didn't have money to waste on staying in this town for

the night, but it was close to ten, and even though I hated to admit it, I didn't feel safe looking around on my own. Once the sun was up, I'd feel more comfortable. People couldn't hide so easily in the daylight.

The inn's small parking lot was mostly full of cars, and my grip eased from around the steering wheel.

At least, something here looked normal.

I parked my car and crossed the street, struck again by how similar the buildings were in color and structure. In Kentucky cities, buildings were a mix of brick, stucco, glass, and whatever of different colors. There wasn't such a uniform feeling. This place, though, wasn't about individuality.

As I approached, the dark walnut double doors opened to reveal a man in his mid-twenties wearing a maroon bellhop outfit. His ash-brown hair hung to his shoulders, and his mesmerizing cognac eyes washed over me. "Hello, miss. Welcome to Shadow Terrace Inn." He lifted his hat, bringing my attention to his smooth porcelain-like skin.

"Hi." This whole town made me feel like I'd gone back in time. "Thank you."

"Of course." He stepped aside.

A light warning tingled inside me, but it had to be left-over paranoia from meeting Creeper back at the bar. This guy seemed friendly, and I was in a freaking hotel where he worked. It wasn't like he would do something shady, especially while on the clock.

Unlike the dark and gothic bar, the hotel interior had lights and beige walls that brightened the room. The lobby wasn't spacious like most of the hotels I'd stayed at—it was about the size of my bedroom. Light hardwood floors creaked with my every step, hinting at their age. The dark walnut reception desk sat opposite the matching front doors with a woman who didn't look much older than me behind it.

She looked up, and her dark russet eyes focused on me as her burgundy hair cascaded over her shoulders. She tapped a pen against the desk. She fidgeted in her seat, and the buttons on her white shirt bulged across her huge breasts. Yet another gorgeous person living in this city.

She arched her eyebrows. "Hi. Are you looking for a room tonight?"

"Yeah, I am." Crap, what if they didn't have any rooms available? I hadn't thought that far ahead.

"Okay. One bed or two?" She pulled out a notebook and licked the tip of her finger before thumbing through the pages.

I almost asked where their computer was but bit back the words.

Whew. My filter had kicked back in. Not minding my words could get me into loads of trouble.

"Just one." I walked over to the desk, realizing that the room and walls were bare. There were no pictures or furniture to encourage people to hang out in the area.

She scribbled on a piece of paper then opened a drawer and removed a key. "Okay, here you go. Room 201." She gestured toward a front corner of the room where a staircase rose against the wall. "Go up one flight, and it'll be the first room on the right. Kieran will bring your luggage up if you give him the keys to your car."

I wouldn't give a stranger the keys to my car even if I'd had luggage. "No need. I'm wearing what I have."

"Oh." She leaned back in her seat. "Interesting."

"You wouldn't by chance know a girl named Annie who frequently comes to town to visit her boyfriend?" I figured it couldn't hurt to ask.

She shook her head hard, almost comically so. "Nope, not at all. But we get a lot of visitors, so I wouldn't recognize every guest."

I knew she was lying, but I couldn't do anything about it. The prickly feeling from earlier returned, warning me not to push it. I'd listen to my gut; it hadn't steered me wrong. "Okay, cool. Just wondering."

"Sure." She squinted as she pushed the key across the table toward me. "Let me know if you need anything else."

"Will do." No, I wouldn't. Something was off in this town.

I made my way to the stairs, forcing myself to move at a reasonable pace. I didn't want these people to realize how much they unsettled me.

The bellhop pretended to be gazing out the door, but I saw his eyes cut in my direction like he was dissecting my every move.

One step at a time, my feet moved faster and faster until I was jogging to the landing. As I turned down the hallway, I couldn't shake that feeling of being watched, even though I was out of their sight.

With trembling hands, I unlocked the door to my room, hurried inside, then slammed it shut and turned the dead-bolt. I frowned. The deadbolt seemed loose. I added the chain, which looked disturbingly flimsy, then flipped on the lights. The walls were the same beige color as downstairs, and the stringy charcoal carpet was gray. The room was sparsely furnished with a bed and chest of drawers.

I turned the light in the bathroom on and checked inside to ensure I was alone. The bathroom was tiny with a small plastic stand-up shower across from a cream-colored sink. A small toilet sat between them against the back wall.

After breathing out the tension that had filled my body,

I washed my face and cleaned my teeth as best I could, then crawled into the bed, leaving the bedside light on as fatigue hit me hard. Before long, I drifted off to sleep.

A JINGLING NOISE startled me awake. I bolted upright in bed and glanced around the room as tendrils of cold fear spread through me. "Who's there?"

The jingling grew louder, and I realized it was the door handle. It sounded as if someone was desperate to get in.

A flash of darkness out of the corner of my eye added to my growing hysteria. Not only was someone barging in, but the shadow had returned.

Holy shit, I should've gone home.

CHAPTER FOUR

The handle shook so hard I feared it would fall apart. Then something pounded against the door like the person was throwing their shoulder into it. The deadbolt barely locked when I'd gotten here, and the chain was laughable—it was old and had barely stayed together when I'd locked it. I'd only done that to give myself a false sense of security while being here alone.

This person didn't give a damn that other guests were close by. The door cracked. It wouldn't hold much longer. The deafening noise should have alerted everyone on this floor that someone was trying to break into my room.

"I said who is i-it?" I tried to hide my fear, but my voice shook. I froze, praying whoever was out there would walk away and leave me the hell alone.

The person responded by banging against the door even harder as if my terror had made them more desperate to get inside.

Sitting in this bed, I might as well have been wearing a sign that said *kill me*. I closed my eyes, trying to block out the noise and steady my heartbeat. Then I climbed out of bed and searched for a weapon, but there wasn't a damn thing to be found. Hell, even the shadow was missing.

Each time the person crashed into the door, I expected it to swing open, but it must have been sturdier than I'd thought because it held. I rushed to the chest of drawers and opened them one by one, searching for anything useful.

The first three drawers were empty, with not even a Holy Bible in them. What the hell kind of hotel was this? We were in the South, for God's sake.

Now wasn't the time for one of my internal ramblings if I wanted to survive. I almost didn't open the bottom drawer —after all, it was the least likely to hold anything useful— but I did it anyway, and something rolled around. Hope ballooned inside my chest.

I snatched the loose object and was disappointed. Not a weapon, as I'd hoped, but a thin black ink pen someone had left behind. Yeah, what was I going to do, write *die* on the person's forehead and hope my wish came true? Hell, I'd bet I wouldn't even get the word written before they knocked me out.

But it was better than nothing.

Maybe.

I turned toward the door, clutching the pen, and prepared myself for a fight. The lobby had been deserted, apart from the hotel staff, so I wasn't sure who it could be.

I desperately surveyed the room for something else, anything else, but there was nothing. The window was too high to climb out of. I'd never been in a hotel room so bare before. There weren't even any bottles of water they used to rip you off with.

The person slammed into the door again, and it buckled inward. This was it. The next time they crashed into that door, they'd be in here with me.

Dammit, I should've grabbed my keys. I hadn't even considered that until now, desperate to find a better weapon, but it was too late. They'd be bursting through in the next second.

I held the pen's tip as far from me as possible and braced myself for a fight. I knew it was my imagination and due to the black spots in my vision caused by an oncoming panic attack, but the shadow was gathering itself and moving toward me.

I refused to go down without a fight, regardless of how futile it would be.

I tensed, ready for action, but instead of another impact, I heard a loud yelp followed by crashing that grew farther away like someone had been tossed down the stairs.

Had they given up and left? But that didn't seem plausible, not with all the effort they'd put into breaking in.

The shadow vanished from my vision, and I jumped at a quiet knock, followed by an internal *yank*, but I swallowed my gasp. Yeah, this had to be a trap. Make the threat sound as if it had disappeared to get the dumb young girl, who'd come here all alone, to open the door.

Gah, I'd been so stupid. I should've left this peculiar town and stayed somewhere more typical.

"Go away," I said, hoping the tremor in my voice wasn't audible through the door. There was no point in pretending I wasn't here. Whoever was out there knew I was inside; otherwise, they would've left when I'd called out the first time.

"Oh, how I wish I could," a familiar voice growled from the other side. "But alas, here I am."

Alas? Who talked like that? Maybe Alex thought it made him sound cool or something equally ridiculous.

"No one is making you stay, and I didn't ask you to

come here. So leave." Wow, I was being rude, but this was the second time he'd magically appeared to handle something going wrong for me. That was more than a little suspicious, and I'd been around enough iffy people to know some enjoyed playing manipulative games.

"Trust me, I wish I could, but I can't leave unless you come with me." He sighed, and I heard a thump against the wall as he leaned against it. "If I leave, you'll be attacked within minutes. I can't allow that to happen, so I need you to come with me. *Now*."

I hated being told what to do, but my body warmed at his command. Uh ... no. I would not be that girl. Not that there was anything wrong with that if you genuinely enjoyed being ordered around, but I didn't like authority figures. Part of growing up in foster homes, I supposed. "I can take care of myself." Eh ... but could I? I glanced at the wimpy pen in my hand. The worst thing it could do was snap off if I stabbed someone with it or maybe scratch them.

But, dammit, it would be the most painful scratch they'd ever had. I'd make sure of it.

"I'm not saying you can't." His tone softened. "I'm saying you shouldn't have to. Will you please open the door?"

Wow, the cocky arrogance and boyish charm had vanished. He sounded sincere, which stripped some of my defenses and somehow made the *yanking* stronger.

I had two options: The first was to open the door and maybe be attacked, and the second was to ignore him and hope he didn't force his way into the room anyway. Either way, if he was the bad guy, I'd wind up in the same precarious situation. But if I played along, I'd have a chance to incapacitate him and get away. That alone made my decision. I was a survivor after all.

A chill ran down my spine from the memories of the near misses with the shadow I'd had when I was younger, and not because of the annoyingly sexy man standing outside my door. I'd been close to doing horrible things before Eliza and Annie had found me.

"Fine, but are you sure it's safe?" Now I was trying to force my voice to tremble, but the sad truth was I didn't need to try. I was scared.

He blew a raspberry. "Yes, Veronica. It's safe. For now."

Straightening my back, I marched across the room, feigning confidence. Inside, I was a floundering mess, but I'd learned from experience if I *appeared* sure of myself, no one questioned me. They didn't want to inspect too deeply in case they found something that made them uncomfortable.

God forbid they might have to help me.

I opened the door, and my breath caught in my lungs. Even though I'd seen him just an hour or two ago, I'd forgotten how gorgeous he was. Words left me, and I stood there gawking at him.

His brows furrowed as he examined me from head to toe. "Are you okay?"

"Yeah." My voice squeaked, revealing my nerves. My reaction wasn't from fear but rather from his proximity. I cleared my throat, taking a moment to regain some composure before continuing. "I was asleep, and someone tried to get into my room."

"They won't be a problem any longer." His jaw twitched, and he glanced over his shoulder at the stairs. "I handled it."

"Like you did the creeper at the bar. Who was it anyways?" A warning rang in my head. "Wait ... why are you here?" He'd stayed behind at the bar with his girlfriend.

How had he followed me when I'd driven my car? Yes, I'd traveled straight through downtown, but I'd been driving a tad faster than I should've been because I'd been eager to get away from that horrid place.

"I was on my way home to a nearby city and noticed your car in the parking lot." He frowned as he entered the hotel room without invitation. "That's when I realized you were a naughty girl and hadn't gone home like I'd told you to."

"News flash." I wasn't sure which version of him I hated more—the flirt, the entitled playboy, or the grump. "You aren't my daddy, so you have no say over my life."

That flirty grin flitted across his face. "I'd be open to being your daddy for at least one go."

"Get out." Anger bled through my words despite my warming body. I gestured to the hallway. "Now."

"Not happening." He strolled into the middle of the room and crossed his arms. "This is the second time tonight I've caught someone trying to take advantage of you. I won't leave until I've escorted you to your car and watched you leave this town."

"I'm not leaving until I find my sister." Shit, there was no telling what had happened to her. She could be in Creeper's underground basement, chained to the stone wall.

"Well, you won't find her tonight." He nodded to the door, which had a huge crack down the center. "And you can't stay here."

"I'll request a new room." Everything inside me screamed to leave, but I couldn't. The way things were going, sleeping in my car wouldn't be much safer. At least in the hotel, there were other people around. "Easy solution."

"You are impossible." He gritted his teeth. "Do I need to carry you to your car for you to get the message?"

"Why don't you want me here?" If he didn't want to be around me, he didn't have to be. "You came here, remember? Go back to *Gwen* and leave me be."

"It's not safe for you here." He ran his fingers through his hair and pulled on the ends.

"I gathered that." I wasn't an idiot even if he thought I was. "Which means it isn't safe for Annie either. What kind of person would leave their sister behind when they know she could be in danger?"

"Dammit." His shoulders sagged, and he closed his eyes as he pinched the bridge of his nose. "You're not leaving, are you?"

I was pretty sure I'd made that clear. "If you try to make me, I'll turn back around and come back. Annie is my family. I have to find her."

"Fine, but can I take you somewhere safer?" He opened his eyes and stepped toward me. "It's truly not safe for you here."

Whoa. That had escalated quickly. "I'm not going home with you." He had a girlfriend, for Christ's sake.

"You're misunderstanding." He waved the sentiment away as if he couldn't be bothered. "I have an acquaintance who owes me a few favors. She and her ma—boyfriend have a house you can stay in safely."

"You want me to stay with someone you know?" This had to be a horrible nightmare I'd wake up from soon. I pinched my arm hard and winced.

His face twisted in confusion. "Why did you just hurt yourself?"

Okay, not a dream. And damn, that hurt. My fingernail

had pinched through the skin, and a bit of blood trickled down my arm. "I was trying something."

"You're bleed—" His face turned pale, and he stumbled away. His nostrils flared as he covered his nose and mouth with his hands.

Out of every scenario I might have imagined, I hadn't expected blood to make him squeamish. "Yeah, sorry." I walked past him into the bathroom and dabbed the cut with toilet paper. I didn't want him to pass out. Then I'd have to protect us both if whoever had tried to break in came back.

With that thought, I realized I didn't want to stay here anyway. "Fine, but if I'm uncomfortable around them, I'm finding another hotel." Even though I wanted to find Annie, I couldn't put myself in danger.

"Deal." He hurried into the hallway, putting distance between us. "We will take your car, and I will grab a cab from there."

Yeah, this would be a very interesting ride.

———

WE'D BEEN DRIVING for ten minutes, retracing the path I'd taken toward the terrace, on the same barren back road that went on for miles. I had to grip the steering wheel hard so I wouldn't lean toward him. The yanking increased with every passing minute, and I wanted to crawl into his lap. But I refused to be another one of his conquests.

"If we don't get there soon, I'm turning around." My hands tightened around the wheel again. He'd conned me into getting into the car with him, and now I was driving us far away from anyone who could help me if things went bad.

He chuckled. "We're here."

My headlights beamed on a sign that said WELCOME TO SHADOW RIDGE.

"What the hell?" He'd taken me into a whole new city. "This isn't what I agreed to."

"My acquaintance lives here. It's a sister town to Shadow Terrace," he said. "It'll be fine. It's less than twenty minutes away."

I turned down the road and already felt more comfortable as we drove through another quaint downtown area. Like the buildings in Shadow Terrace, most of the structures were brick, but that was where the similarities ended. They were all painted in different colors and didn't stick to one architectural style.

Alex gave me instructions, leading me through the town and into a wooded area with thick cypress trees lining the road. The most reassuring part was that, even at this late hour, we passed other vehicles. It didn't feel like a ghost town with odd couples walking down the streets.

After one more turn, a nice neighborhood full of craftsman-style houses came into view. They all had a uniform look but were painted in varying shades of white, blue, green, and yellow.

"That one right there," Alex said, pointing.

I pulled into the driveway he'd indicated and turned off the car. The home was a white, one-story house with a wrap-around porch. Whoever lived here had enough money to live comfortably.

I used to envy people like that before Eliza and Annie came into my life. Then I'd learned that struggling for money and skimping to get by wasn't such a hardship if you were surrounded by people you loved.

"Come on." Alex jogged to the front door and rang the bell.

"Hey." I couldn't believe he'd just done that. There were no lights on, so they had to be asleep. "Why didn't you call first?" I whispered, hoping not to wake the neighbors too.

He smirked and tilted his head. "That's cute but calling them and ringing the doorbell would result in the same thing."

The front door swung open, and a tall, handsome man glared at Alex. His hazel eyes darkened to substantially black, and his honey-brown hair flopped into his face. He stepped into Alex's personal space, emphasizing the approximately six inches in height he had on him, and straightened his shoulders. His bare chest somehow seemed even more muscular. "What the fuck are you doing here?"

At least, he had on black pajama bottoms, or this would've been more uncomfortable.

When he'd said *acquaintance*, I'd assumed they were friendly. This guy didn't want us here, and I had no clue how to respond.

CHAPTER FIVE

I turned to Alex and chuckled without humor, allowing malice to shine through. "You brought me to stay with people you expect to help me but clearly don't like you?" I'd known he was arrogant, but this went way beyond that.

He was entitled, a trait I despised.

Entitled people had the world handed to them on a silver platter or expected to be compensated for the struggles they were forced to overcome. I didn't want to rely on anyone, despite my shitty upbringing.

Being self-sufficient and taking care of the people I loved were the most important things in my life.

No one owed me anything.

"At least, she gets it." The man waved a hand at me. "And she's just met me. What the hell is your excuse?"

Alex scowled at me. "You're not helping matters. Stay quiet."

"What did you just say to me?" I placed a hand on my chest in horror.

"Griffin, calm down," a soft female voice said from inside the house. Then one of the most beautiful girls I'd ever seen stepped up beside the man. Her long silver hair fell across her face, making her purple-silver eyes stand out against her light olive complexion and the white robe she was wrapped in. She was practically the same height as Alex, and there was something about her that settled me.

Her attention locked on me, and she sniffed. "Obviously, something is going on, so let's hear them out." She flicked her gaze at the man, and something crossed his face as if they'd communicated without words.

Wow. They were about my age, but they gave the impression of having been together for a long time.

"I'm here to cash in one of those favors." Alex stepped closer to me, possessively. We were so close our arms brushed, and my skin tingled.

"You fucking prick," Griffin growled.

"What are you asking for?" The girl stood straight with an air of authority surrounding her. Even in her yoga pants and shirt, she came off as a leader.

Alex smiled charmingly. "I need Veronica to stay with you until I can convince her to go home."

"I don't want to be an inconvenience." The last thing I wanted was to stay where I wasn't welcomed. Lord knew I'd done that enough with the foster homes I'd been placed in. So many of those people fostered kids for the money and didn't take care of them. "I can figure something out. It's no big deal."

"There you go." Griffin began to shut the front door. "She can figure something out."

"Wait." Alex caught the door, preventing him from shutting it on us. "Hear me out."

This guy didn't know when to quit. "Will you stop? They obviously don't like you or want me here. Why the hell are you trying to dump me on them?" I pivoted toward him and put a hand on my hip.

"Oh, I don't know." Alex's flirty demeanor was nowhere in sight as his breathing turned shallow. "Maybe because you were attacked twice in one night. Once in your own hotel room."

"Which is not their problem." I wanted to punch something. No, I wanted to punch *him*. "Or yours, for that matter."

He lifted his chin and glared down his nose at me. "You don't think I know that? Of course, it's not my problem."

Asshole. "Then why are you making it your problem?" He didn't get to drag my ass over here and then talk to me like I was an idiot. "Why don't you go give *Gwen* a good time and forget about me?" The words caught in my throat. For some damn reason, the thought infuriated me, and that pissed me off even more.

"Gwen?" Griffin's nose wrinkled in disgust. "Your sister? Dude."

Gwen was his *sister*? So ...not his girlfriend. My face burned, and I fought the urge to cover it with my hands.

"No!" Alex's jaw dropped. He glanced at me, then at the couple still standing in the doorway. "Gwen and I aren't —" He stopped and flailed his hands around. "She just thought we were—"

The girl laughed. "I don't think you're helping yourself."

"Gwen met me at Thirsty's, and Veronica assumed she was my girlfriend." He sighed.

"Nope, you don't get to make me sound crazy." Well, in all fairness, I already sounded crazy, but that wasn't the point. "There were couples making out all over the place in that weird bar. I didn't see a single person other than me and the creep who attacked me. What else was I to assume?" And why was I thrilled that she wasn't his girl-friend? That didn't mean he didn't have one.

"You took your sister to a date place?" Griffin dropped his hand, no longer intent on shutting us out. "What is wrong with you?"

"I was meeting with the bar owner, and she was joining the discussion." Alex's shoulders sagged, his pompous air extinguished. "I can't help it if that's where we..." He trailed off like he was searching for the right words.

Strange. He hadn't had a problem with words until this moment.

"Where the city's couples like to hang out," he finished with a grimace. "There was nothing strange going on."

"Nothing strange?" More of my sanity flew out the door. "Everywhere I looked, there were couples nearly having an orgy, except for you, your sister, and some other strange people who could pass as grim reapers. Oh, and let's not forget about someone attempting to break into my hotel room!"

"Okay." The girl sighed and touched her boyfriend's arm. "She can stay with us."

"What?" Griffin's head snapped in her direction.

She lifted an eyebrow, and they again had a silent conversation.

That both intrigued and scared me. The thought of finding a person who could read my thoughts in the blink of an eye was truly romantic, but I would never want to be that emotionally invested in someone. The thought of losing Annie or Eliza cut too deep and finding someone I had even stronger feelings for might kill me.

"Thank you." He nodded. "But this counts as only one favor. Got it?"

"Yeah, we got it." Griffin stepped out of the doorway and waved me inside. "Where's your stuff? I can get it for you."

"Uh ..." I glanced at my body. "This is all I have, but thanks." After the abrupt meeting, I couldn't believe he offered to help me.

"No problem." The girl took my arm and pulled me inside. "My clothes will be too long, but we can make something work."

"I'm good." The more they went out of their way for me, the more I'd put them out. I wanted to disappear, so they'd forget I was even there. That had worked before. "Thanks, though."

"Here," Alex said as he handed me my keys. "I locked the car."

"Shouldn't I drive you somewhere?" Whether I liked it or not, Alex had helped me twice over. And I didn't get weird vibes from Griffin or his girl, so that made it three times. "I hate to leave you hanging."

"Don't worry about me." He winked. "I'm a big boy and know my way around."

"If you haven't called for an Uber, Griffin can for you," the girl interjected. "You can sit on the porch." She gestured to a black iron table with four chairs around it.

Still, I didn't want to leave him inconvenienced. It felt wrong—proving I was way too emotionally invested in this man, and he needed to go. "Okay, well, thanks again."

"Be careful." He shook his head. "And for the first time since I've met you, don't do something stupid."

The urge to flip him the bird was overwhelming, but I kept the finger caged. Somehow. "Bite me."

He tilted his head and purred, "Well ... if you insist."

"Yeah, nope. I'm not listening to this," Griffin said and shut the door in Alex's face.

Even though he was outside the door, a piece of me *yank*ed from my chest and stayed behind with Alex.

What was wrong with me?

Griffin arched an eyebrow at me.

I felt as if I were under a microscope. "Once he walks away, I'll get out of your hair."

These two seemed like nice people, and I didn't need to drag them into anything. The less they knew about my plans, the easier they could deny their involvement if something bad happened.

"Absolutely not." The girl shook her head and held her hand out. "I'm Sterlyn, by the way."

"Veronica." I shook her hand and almost winced. Her grip was firm. I hadn't expected that, but it seemed fitting, as did her name. "And I'm sorry he had me barge in on you like this."

"If you've been attacked twice, it's best you don't stay alone." She led the way into a cozy living room.

The walls were blue-gray, and a pearl-gray couch that complemented the color scheme sat against the room's longest wall in front of a flat-screen television mounted on the opposite wall. A matching loveseat sat perpendicular to the couch and across from the windows, which were accented with white blinds. To the right of the windows was a doorway that led to their backyard, I assumed.

Homey was the best way to describe the decor, but maybe that was partly due to Sterlyn, who had confidence-instilling pureness pouring off her.

Something about Sterlyn made me trust her, and that scared me. I was warming up to her faster than anyone before. "Yeah, but this is a different city. I can stay at the hotel."

"Sterlyn's right." Griffin walked up to his girlfriend and placed an arm around her shoulders. "You actually seem nice, and we told Alex we'd let you stay here."

"Are you sure?" He hadn't been all that thrilled with Alex bringing me here, but he didn't seem to mind now. I had a feeling that was due to Alex no longer being here. Something bad must have happened between them. I wanted to ask what, but it wasn't my business.

"Positive." Sterlyn kissed Griffin on the cheek. "I'll be back in bed soon. Let me get her settled in the guest room."

"Okay." Griffin pouted but then chuckled.

I followed Sterlyn past the kitchen and down a short hallway to a door on the right. As I stepped into the room, I felt at peace in a way I hadn't at the hotel. The walls were a shade darker than the living room, and a queen-sized bed was centered against one wall, covered with white sheets and a charcoal comforter. A dresser with a television mounted above it sat against the opposite wall. To the right, an open door showed an empty walk-in closet.

"Does this work for you?" Sterlyn stopped in the center of the room and spun around. "If not, there's another room across the hall, but this is the bigger of the two rooms."

I came close to laughing but realized she was serious. If I didn't like it, she really would show me the other room. "This is perfect unless you want me to take the smaller room."

"No need." She sat on the edge of the bed. "It's just Griffin and me here, at least for now. Sometimes, one of our friends sleeps over, but they can take the other room if it comes to that."

"Oh, I don't plan to stay here long." That had felt like

an open-ended invitation. "I just need to find my sister and get us back home."

"Your sister is here?" Her brows furrowed. "Why aren't you staying with her?"

I filled her in on the story. "I think something bad happened to her. I don't know how to explain it, but ... she snuck down here to visit the university, met this guy, and kept sneaking back because he constantly harasses her. She's become secretive, has stopped answering my calls, and is ignoring my texts. It's like she's changed overnight."

Sterlyn's face tensed. "When did she first visit? Do you remember?"

"In April." It was hard to believe that time had moved so fast, but I needed Sterlyn to understand how long this had been going on. "Why?"

"No reason." She tried to smile, but it didn't reach her eyes. "I'm sure you'll find her in the morning. The best thing you can do is get some rest. Let me grab you some clothes."

"Seriously, you don't need to do that." I should've brought my own change of clothes. I wasn't sure why I hadn't. Even if I'd found Annie, it would've taken another five hours to get home. We probably would've stayed overnight anyway. But I'd been so worried I'd run out of the house, determined to get down here. "I'm fine sleeping in my shirt or naked."

"I insist." She walked out the doorway, clearly on a mission.

Not sure what to do, I strolled across the room and peeked out the window. Their backyard was a decent size and backed up against the woods. The house next to them had a pool in the backyard, and I raised a brow when I saw there was no fence around it. The entire view was breathtaking with a half-moon high in the sky shining down on it all.

"Here you go," Sterlyn said, startling me.

Spinning to face her, I clutched my chest. My heart pounded. I hadn't heard her walk back in. "Oh, thanks."

"You don't need to be scared. You're safe here. That house you were just looking at is our best friend's place who is trained in protecting people." She placed yoga pants and a shirt on the bed. "Anyways, feel free to wear these, and there are spare toothbrushes and toothpaste in the bathroom. Do you need anything else?"

"This is more than enough." I hadn't planned on changing, but I felt dirty in these clothes. I wasn't sure if it was from the attack or something stirring inside me. "Thank you."

"Good night." She walked to the door and paused. "If you need anything, just holler or walk down the hallway. Our room is at the very end of the hallway, so we'll be close by."

"Okay, thank you."

She shut the door, and I quickly changed into the clothes she'd left behind. She had a good five inches on me, and it was easy to tell when I put her yoga pants on. They hung down on the shaggy brown carpet, so I rolled them up until they hit me at the ankles.

It didn't matter. I was only sleeping in them. I crawled into bed and, within seconds, fell asleep.

I woke up and blinked several times, trying to remember where the hell I was. Dreams filled with darkness and shadows had plagued me all night.

I squinted against the daylight pouring through the window. I hadn't bothered to draw the blinds. I looked around at the charcoal comforter and noticed a few pictures of Griffin, Sterlyn, and a few other people on the dresser that had to be their friends. They all appeared happy in the woods, sitting next to some irises.

The entire night before crept back into my brain. Of course, my mind went straight to *him*. The aggravating, sexy man who was bad news.

And Annie.

I sat up quickly, the urge to find her slamming back inside me.

I rolled out of bed and changed then made the bed and folded the pajamas. After placing them on the end of the bed, I hurried through a brief morning wash in the bathroom then found my way to the kitchen. Sterlyn was already there, dressed in jeans and a burnt-orange shirt, scrambling eggs on the stove.

"Hey, I'm heading out." They had to be getting ready to go themselves. "I didn't mean to sleep so late."

"It's fine." She smiled. "I'm making us breakfast. I hope you like eggs and bacon."

"Love it." I didn't want to be ungracious and turn down their food.

"So ... what are your plans for today?"

The way she asked made my skin crawl. There was a tenseness to her eyes, telling me it wasn't a casual question despite her tone.

She wanted to know what I was going to do ... but why? Maybe she wasn't so harmless after all.

CHAPTER SIX

A smart-ass retort sat on the tip of my tongue, but I swallowed it. She didn't deserve sarcasm after taking me in, even if the only reason she'd allowed me to stay was that she owed Alex favors.

"You know what I have to do." There was no point in lying. I had to get back to Shadow Terrace and find Annie. Every second that ticked by could put her in more danger. On top of that, I was ready to leave.

Okay, that was a stretch. The thought of not seeing Alex again bothered me a little too much, which meant getting distance from him was for the best. He already took up too much space in my mind, even though I'd known him for less than a day.

Way too much damn space.

"Do you have any idea where to start?" She spooned out the eggs, dividing them among three plates.

"No, but I'll figure it out." Thirsty's had been my only clue. Annie hadn't discussed any other places except for her boyfriend's house, and I had no idea where that was. Everything appeared so similar anyway. All I knew was that he lived close to the river. It narrowed down the location, but not enough.

She sighed and placed three pieces of bacon on one plate. "After being attacked twice, do you think it's smart to just wing it?"

I didn't like the direction this conversation was taking. What was it with people trying to talk me out of finding Annie? I had figured that a fellow woman would understand. "I can't leave her. She's my sister and my best friend."

"Whoa." She lifted a hand. "I'm not saying don't look for her. I was just thinking that if you don't know where to go from here, maybe you should start at the university, especially if that's where she met him." She picked up a plate and handed it to me.

That was a solid idea. I took the plate and tried to keep my voice level. Obviously, my annoyance had bled through. "You're right. Maybe she'll be there with him." It bothered me that I hadn't considered that.

"Exactly." She smiled and picked up the last two plates then led me to the round table with five chairs around it.

I sat across from where she'd put down her plate and Griffin's. "Do you have coffee?"

"Of course." She chuckled. "It's next to the refrigerator. You can find the k-cups underneath the coffeemaker, in the cabinet. There's creamer in the refrigerator."

I didn't need creamer. I liked my coffee black and as strong as possible. My mind felt fuzzy, which was probably why I hadn't thought about searching for Annie at the university. If I didn't get my brain in gear, I'd make foolish mistakes and prolong my trip. And the more time Annie spent with that asshole, the deeper he could sink his claws into her. Even though I hoped she'd leave with me willingly,

I was worried she might not be happy about it and want to stay with the prick.

I refused to think about the worst possible alternative because a world without Annie in it didn't make sense to me.

Ugh, I had to take it one step at a time. I couldn't jump to conclusions. But I couldn't help it. I worried about shit. Something inside me always took my thoughts to a dark level.

Forcing my legs to move, I went to the machine and made myself a cup of coffee. As I headed back to the table to eat, Griffin came in and sat down. His honey-brown hair was gelled back, giving him a put-together look that was topped with a wrinkle-free navy blue shirt and tan slacks. He smiled warmly at Sterlyn, making the gold flecks in his eyes noticeable, before flicking his attention to me, and his face turned into a mask of indifference.

He didn't want me here, but Sterlyn seemed determined to help me.

In other words, breakfast was going to be interesting.

AFTER I'D FINISHED the last bite on my plate and brought it to the sink, Griffin cleared his throat. "So ... are you heading back home or hanging around town for a little while longer?" The edge in his voice caught me off guard. He sounded worried, but I wasn't sure why the hell he'd care.

"Actually ..." Sterlyn fidgeted in her seat, which also seemed out of line with her character. She'd given off a strong, steadfast vibe, but at this moment, she came off as nervous. "Veronica and I were talking earlier, and she's decided to come with us to Shadow Ridge University to search for her sister."

"What?" Griffin asked, sounding shocked. "Are you serious?"

Wow. He wasn't the warmest toward me, but he *really* didn't want me hanging out at the university. I got that it was an exclusive institution, but it wasn't like I was applying to go there.

"Is that a problem?" I faced him and forced my hands to stay at my sides instead of placing them on my hips like I wanted. His arrogance was stifling.

"Not at all," Sterlyn answered for him, irritating me.

"Look, I like you." And the problem was I actually did. I felt connected to her in a strange way that didn't make sense and was also terrifying. Thankfully, it wasn't the lustful, dirty thoughts that consumed my mind with Alex but a more familial connection. "But I like to know where I stand with people." I pointed at Griffin. "He doesn't like me, but I want to hear him say it."

People usually told the truth when they were put on the spot.

"No, that's not it." Griffin ran a hand through his gelled hair, messing it a little and making him appear less snooty. "If you want honesty, I'll give it to you. I don't trust Alex, and him bringing you here makes me wary of you." His jaw twitched.

"You'd be stupid not to feel that way." Hell, I didn't even trust the strange, sexy man. "You're smart, but I feel like your distrust goes beyond that." Griffin was leveling with me, making me warm up to him a little. It wasn't personal, and I was okay with that as long as it was the truth. "Any other reasons?"

He locked eyes with me. "Alex is it."

If someone lied, they avoided your gaze, so there was that. "I'm not here to screw you over or get dirt for Alex." If they were being honest, I would be too. It was only fair. "And I have no interest in hurting anyone. There're enough shitty people in the world, and I'm not one of them."

He nodded and blew out a breath. "That's fair."

"See, I told you." Sterlyn arched an eyebrow and stood from her chair. "She isn't part of whatever the hell Alex has going on. If I thought she was, I wouldn't have agreed to let her stay."

"How can you be so sure?" I was shooting myself in the foot, but how the hell could she be so confident? "I could be saying what you want to hear to gain your trust or so you won't watch me as carefully."

She winked as she picked up her plate. "Oh, you're not doing that. Let's just say I have a sixth sense."

Everyone I'd met since arriving at Shadow Terrace talked in riddles. Something was different about this place, but it didn't matter. All I needed to do was find Annie and leave all this craziness behind. "Well, okay then."

"I need to make a few phone calls before we leave," Griffin said. He scratched his nose while discreetly cutting his eyes to Sterlyn. "I'll be back in a minute." He passed me and stuck his plate in the sink before heading toward their bedroom.

"If you give me directions to the university, I can head on over." I turned on the water and started washing Griffin's and my plates.

"You can ride with us." She smiled and placed her plate on the counter beside the sink. "We're all going to the same place."

"How long are you staying there?" I wanted to figure

everything out before we needed to leave. Hopefully, people at the university would be willing to help me.

"I work on campus at the coffee shop, but Carter will let me take a break to bring you back here when you're ready to leave. He's all about rules and making sure everyone takes their breaks even when we're short-handed."

Trying not to be rude, I kept my mouth shut and thought through my response as I finished cleaning her plate and set all three of them on the drainboard. "But you wouldn't have to do that if I drove." I didn't want to depend on them or relinquish control.

"Well, I was trying to be nice, but you're forcing my hand." She leaned against the counter. "The university has designated visiting days. Any other day, if you don't have a key card to get through the gate, you aren't getting in. So if you want to look for your sister there, you're kind of stuck riding with us."

And there it was. Of course, the school didn't let just anyone in. Damn snobby places. "Okay." I didn't have a choice. Like Sterlyn had said, this was the most solid plan. If I could find Annie at the university or find a lead to her boyfriend's house, that would be better than going back to check Thirsty's. The thought of stepping into that bar again wasn't appealing.

"Great." She snatched the pans off the stove and moved over to clean them.

"I got this." It was the least I could do since she'd made breakfast. "Go do whatever you need to do and let me know when it's time to go."

Something flickered across her face, and she patted my arm. My blood revved up at her touch, but I tried not to overanalyze it.

"Don't take Griffin personally. He's very protective of

those he loves." Tenderness crept into her eyes. "We've had it rough these past few months, so he's grown jaded."

Hell, so was I. Maybe he and I had more in common than I'd like to consider. "It's fine. You could stand to be more cautious too."

"If I'd gotten a bad vibe from you, you wouldn't have made it through the front door." She smirked. "Let's just say I'm an excellent judge of character."

I believed that. "So, you think Alex is an asshole too?" Maybe if she told me horrible stories about the guy, I could get him out of my head. I'd seen my fair share of egotistical assholes and jerks, and I despised them. I tried to surround myself with good people. So far, I'd found two before Sterlyn: Eliza and Annie. That made my circle extremely small.

"Alex is ... complicated." Sterlyn pursed her lips. "If you'd asked me that yesterday, before you showed up at my door, I would've said hands down yes. But there's something different about him when it comes to you, and I can't put my finger on it. I think he genuinely wants to help you."

Yeah, that didn't help. "I don't know what you think you saw, but I assure you he's an asshole." Now I felt bad. "Well, he's arrogant and selfish, but I guess I shouldn't call him an asshole since he rescued me twice."

"Speaking of which, what happened over there? Like details, not just that you got attacked at the bar and hotel. Was it someone in particular?" She tapped a finger against her bottom lip and watched every move I made.

I finished cleaning the last pan and put it on the rack next to the plates, ignoring the intensity of her stare. I quickly told her about the attacks and glossed over my fear, but my voice shook occasionally.

"I'm glad he brought you here." Her lips mashed together into a line.

The bedroom door opened, and Griffin strode over to us, car keys in hand and a backpack slung over his shoulder. "Are you two ready?"

"Yes," I said too quickly. As soon as I found Annie, I would relax. Annie always teased me about being high strung. When something worried me, I stayed on edge until it was resolved. I wished I could be more like her and remain calm, no matter what I faced.

Something passed between the two of them again, yet another silent conversation. I wasn't too uncomfortable except that their expressions were strained and not lustful.

"Let's go," Sterlyn said, emphasizing each word, as though answering an unspoken question. "She needs to find her sister."

I'd thought Griffin and I had come to an understanding at the end of breakfast, but maybe we hadn't. He again wasn't thrilled about me joining them at the university. I wanted to comment, but I didn't want to be left behind.

"Okay." He walked past us to a door that probably led to the garage, but he paused and turned back to me. "But there will be some ground rules while we're there. We're risking a lot by bringing you, and you can't cause any problems. Someone needs to be with you at all times."

Anger pooled in my stomach. I wouldn't stand here and be talked to like that.

CHAPTER SEVEN

My arms trembled with unbridled anger. All my life, people had talked down to me as if I wasn't worthy of respect or love, and dammit, I'd learned that I was.

He walked out the door, and I hurried to follow him when an arm looped through mine, holding me back.

"Hey, I promise that wasn't what you think it was." Sterlyn gestured toward him. "There are things going on that you aren't aware of, and he's under a lot of stress. Us taking you to the school could cause problems."

Sure, we'd pretend that was the case, but I could tell he didn't want me to tag along. "Then why did you suggest it?"

Her eyes deepened to a lavender. "Because if I were in your shoes, nothing would stop me from finding my family member."

"True." My voice cracked, conveying my emotions. Annie was my sister by all rights. "But I don't want to cause problems for you two either. I can find a way onto campus myself."

"No, you need to come with us." She tugged me toward the garage. "It'll be better that way."

I wanted to argue, but Sterlyn was determined that I go with them, and I wondered why. If this sped up the process and I didn't have to lurk around to find a way in, I'd play along. I didn't need the cops catching me trespassing. Sterlyn and Griffin were adults, and they had made their decision, even if begrudgingly.

A high-end black Navigator sat in their garage. Griffin obviously came from money. Sterlyn and I went to the passenger side of the vehicle, and I climbed into the back. The damn thing was fully loaded. It even had seat warmers. I wished it was cold outside so I could warm my buns to a toasty level.

Griffin clutched the steering wheel, his knuckles white, but I ignored him.

We pulled out of the garage and drove through the neighborhood, heading toward my destination. My heart pounded. Part of me hoped that Annie was there, but I was afraid of what I might find.

The sun rose over the tree line as we drove through the quaint downtown. The two-lane road was lined with brick buildings that connected for miles. Unlike Shadow Terrace, cars were parked up and down the streets, and people walked along the sidewalks, going to work. There were restaurants, banks, and a movie theater—everything you'd expect to find in a thriving Tennessee town.

We breezed through the downtown area, stopping at a few of the lights. People milled across the street, and a sizable family headed into an establishment called Sniffers' Restaurant.

I fidgeted in my seat, trying to keep my mouth shut, but between Alex being on my brain constantly and my desperation to see him, I lost the battle. "So ... things seemed tense between you two and Alex. How did you wind up owing him favors?"

Griffin tensed.

Yeah, I should've stayed quiet.

"Griffin and I hold important positions in our community, as do Alex and his family. We're on the council—that's the local government." Sterlyn glanced over her shoulder at me and paused as if she were choosing her words carefully. "Someone Griffin trusted betrayed him, and we were attacked. Alex stepped up to help us and got his older brother, Matthew, to assist in calming the situation down."

Ugh, I hated politics. I'd seen plenty of people backstabbing each other on television. "He does have an air of authority about him. But that doesn't explain the animosity." And his demeanor was both alluring and infuriating.

Sexy bastard.

"His brother is the head of Shadow Terrace, and because of that, Alex has a lot of influence." She chewed on her bottom lip. "But they only helped us to further their own agenda, and that's how we wound up owing them favors, even though we didn't ask for their help."

Damn, would he use that tactic on me? He had helped me twice and found me a place to stay.

My mind reeled as we turned toward the woods and flowing river. Just over the treetops, about a mile away, several towering brick buildings set close together came into view. They looked maybe a couple of years old.

Sterlyn motioned to the buildings. "That's the university."

I remembered Annie telling me that, despite the school being new, it had been named one of the best universities in the United States. Its quick rise through the ranks had many coveting a spot at the school, especially for their law program.

Griffin turned onto the road to the university, which was secured by a black wrought iron gate. We pulled up next to the guard shack set between the entrance and exit.

The gate was closed, and Griffin stopped and rolled down his window. The guard saluted Griffin as he pulled out a key card and swiped it against the reader. The gate clicked and slowly opened.

"Thanks, Gerald," Griffin said and pulled forward.

Redbuds, poplars, and sycamore trees lined the road toward a brick building that was at least a hundred yards long and two stories high. In front was a grassy greenway with several empty benches, except for the one close to the double doors where a girl sat reading a textbook. It was approaching eight in the morning, which I supposed was too early by student standards.

As we got closer, the road curved right toward a parking lot with a few cars sprinkled throughout.

Griffin parked in the reserved spot closest to the building. Of *course*, he'd have his own special parking spot.

"Where do I find the main office?" I had a feeling it wasn't open yet, but I could locate it before there was a line.

"It's in the same building as the coffee shop." Sterlyn opened her door and climbed out. "The one right in front of us. It doesn't open until nine, but you can hang out with me in the shop until then."

At least, I wouldn't be walking around the campus aimlessly in search of the right place. "I'll try the office first then maybe stroll around. Annie could show up anywhere." Annie wasn't a coffee drinker, which still disappointed me. People who didn't like coffee couldn't be trusted. Well, no one except her.

"No," Sterlyn said forcefully before she cleared her throat and regrouped.

What was *up* with their attitude about me being here? I'd already told them I could have snuck in on my own. I didn't want to be tied to them and unable to search for Annie. "You know why I'm here—" I opened my door and exited the vehicle.

"Look, I didn't mean it like that." She sighed. "There are ... people here whose radar you don't want to be on. It'll be best if you get her boyfriend's address and go to his house instead of searching for her here and drawing attention. I doubt he'd bring her here anyway because she isn't a student yet even if she is a contender."

I hadn't thought of it like that, but she was right. If Annie knew she shouldn't be here, she wouldn't come. She was a huge rule follower and often kept me out of trouble. "Fine, but what the hell am I supposed to do?"

"We're down a person in the coffee shop if you want to help out. Someone in the kitchen called in sick," she said. "You'd get paid."

Agh, she had me at *paid*. Even though I had a job, we were always tight on money. Making extra cash wouldn't hurt. We caught up with Griffin, who had a frown etched onto his face. I was pretty sure it was permanent or would be until I left.

The three of us walked down the sidewalk toward the front of the building. The girl sitting on the bench sniffed loudly and dropped her book. Huge dark eyes locked on me, and she licked her lips hungrily. "What do we have here?" she cooed.

"A visitor." Griffin stepped in front of me, stiffening. "Who is protected by me."

Protected? What an odd thing to say. *Invited* would've made a hell of a lot more sense.

"Come on, Veronica." Sterlyn grabbed my arm and dragged me to the door. Griffin and the girl spoke so quietly I couldn't make out a damn thing they were saying. I wanted to eavesdrop, but Sterlyn's hold wouldn't give.

"Ronnie," I murmured distractedly. "My friends call me Ronnie." Oh, shit. I'd given her permission to call me by my nickname.

Instead of making it awkward, she opened the door, and I gave up trying to overhear Griffin's conversation. I stepped into the building to find standard beige walls and a forest-brown tile floor. A hallway to the right had signs for admissions, tuition, financial aid, and all the various administrative departments needed for a college of this size. "This is where I need to be at nine?"

"Yes, and we'll be here in the meantime." She pointed at a bookstore with an attached coffee shop. To the left was a cafeteria with seating out front. Students were eating breakfast.

My stomach growled even though I'd eaten not even an hour ago.

A student carrying a tray passed us and stopped in his tracks to inspect me. His brows furrowed, but he continued moving, dropping off his tray and going out some glass doors to picnic tables that overlooked the woods and the river.

Did I have a sign that said I wasn't worthy of attending here? What was it with all these people staring at me? I hadn't thought I stuck out that much, but everyone here could sense I didn't belong. Maybe *reject* or *loser* was stamped on my forehead.

It didn't matter. I only had to endure it for a little while. Besides, I'd been judged before.

"Come on." Sterlyn turned toward the coffee shop.

Grateful for the distraction, I hurried into the shop and passed by a table occupied by a group of gorgeous girls. Just like everyone else, they all turned toward me and stopped their conversation. The one closest to me wrinkled her nose and glanced at Sterlyn. "Is today a visitation day? We didn't get the memo."

"Something like that," Sterlyn replied without slowing.

The girl scoffed. "Then why weren't we notified?"

This whole situation was crazy. Was the school so small that everyone knew each other?

"Because it's none of your damn business," Sterlyn spat as she slid behind the counter and pushed buttons on the cash register. "Ronnie, why don't you come back here with me? I can get you set up."

Ready to get away from prying eyes, I followed her through the white swinging doors between the cash register and expresso machines.

"It's about damn time you got here." An attractive guy close to twenty stood in front of a counter with various types of bread spread about. His shaggy brown hair hung in his eyes and sweat beaded on his forehead. A deep frown marred his face as he opened the microwave and removed two eggs. He stilled as his head lifted and his frown somehow deepened. "Who is she?"

Wow. He'd spoken as if I weren't even in the room. "I'm Veronica. And you are?" If he wanted to give me attitude, I could dish it back.

The corners of Sterlyn's mouth tipped upward as she attempted to hide a smile. "Look, I had to bring her. I was hoping she could work back here for the morning. I'm guessing we're short a person."

"I don't know ..." He plopped the eggs onto a plain bagel and placed his hands on the table. "I could—"

"If you don't want my help, that's fine." I'd figure something out. Maybe I could hang out in the Navigator until the office opened. Granted, considering the way Griffin had treated me, he'd probably worry that I'd steal the vehicle. They all gaped at me in a way that made it clear I wasn't one of them.

"Carter," Sterlyn said warningly. "Do I need to remind you—"

"No, you don't." He huffed and crossed his arms. "I swear you put me in precarious situations all the damn time."

"You decided to give Deissy another chance." Sterlyn gestured to me. "I figured she wouldn't show up and we could use a hand back here. Unless you'd rather I make the drinks."

"God no." His eyes popped from his head. "You're awful at it."

"Then you can work the cash register *and* the espresso machine." Sterlyn grabbed clear gloves and prepared to put them on and work in the kitchen. "That's fine."

"That bitch Deissy had to put me in this position," he grumbled and snatched the gloves from Sterlyn. "If I do this, you keep me out of trouble. All right?"

She placed a hand on her chest. "You have my word."

"Why would you get in trouble? Just pay me under the table." They were making this much too complicated. "Problem solved."

"Great idea," Sterlyn replied quickly. "We hadn't considered that. That's exactly what we'll do." She gave me a rundown about the breads and how long to cook each egg, and then she showed me where the bacon, sausage, and cheese were stored in the refrigerator. Once she'd run through everything, she grabbed Carter's arm along with the egg bagel he'd made and pulled him out the door, leaving me alone.

I took a deep breath and enjoyed the solitude. Back here, I was safe from scrutiny.

———————

TIME ZIPPED by as I made order after order. Sterlyn and I worked well as a team. Being busy gave my mind a reprieve from worrying about Annie and everything weird going on.

I glanced at the clock above the door and realized the front office would open in just ten minutes. Ugh, that meant I would have to deal with more stares. Hell, the longer I stayed here, the more unsettled I felt, despite Shadow Ridge *appearing* normal. Something ... odd hovered in the air, though I hadn't picked up on it in Shadow Ridge until we'd gotten to the university.

Annie had been determined to come here after getting back home, talking about the amazing campus and stellar classes. Of course, her boyfriend had added to her excitement. I couldn't imagine her being thrilled with the attention I'd gotten just walking in the doors. Things continued to not add up. Annie was smart. Why would she subject herself to this?

The clock struck nine, and I finished the last bacon egg sandwich and placed it on a tray.

Something *yank*ed inside me, and a familiar voice growled loud enough that I heard it all the way in the back. "What the hell, Sterlyn? You were supposed to send her home, not bring her to campus!" Footsteps grew louder as he made his way toward me.

Alex was here, and he was pissed. But he had no right to be.

I straightened my shoulders, ready to confront him.

CHAPTER EIGHT

My heart rate increased, and I wasn't sure if it was from annoyance or because I was about to see him, which infuriated me. It was likely a combination of the two, but I shouldn't have been excited to see his perfectly sculpted face again.

Damn him.

"For the love of God," Carter complained. "We have a huge line. Can you two argue later?"

"Fine. I'll solve the problem," Alex retorted, and then his voice grew loud. "Anyone who doesn't want to piss off a council member, get out of here *now*."

"Alex," Sterlyn warned. "You're making a scene."

That didn't surprise me. Alex was a force, and despite not knowing him long, I could tell he was used to getting his way. That had to be why he was so angry.

"You don't think you've done that by bringing her here?" he spat. "How do you think I knew about it?"

"No one has to leave," Sterlyn said just as loudly, authority ringing in her voice. "But I do need to talk to Alex, so a little patience would be nice."

"Just ... go back in the kitchen." Carter sighed. "I'll take care of the orders and drinks while you sort this shit out."

The door swung inward, and Alex marched into the kitchen. His eyes locked on mine, and he made a beeline for me. My heart almost felt complete again.

Like the missing piece had returned.

Whoa. That emotion was way too intense for someone I'd met less than twenty-four hours ago. What was wrong with me? Well, that was a loaded question that could take all day to answer, but that wasn't the point.

His face was so tense that his jaw twitched. When he reached my side, his shoulders relaxed marginally, but if I hadn't been watching him so intently, I wouldn't have noticed. He tugged at the collar of his cobalt V-neck shirt, which contrasted with his eyes. His jeans hugged his body in ways that put my mind in the gutter. My hand itched to grab his ass.

Yup, something was definitely wrong with me.

"You weren't supposed to do anything stupid," he hissed as he stepped closer to me, his sweet smell clouding my mind.

That was enough to clear up the haze. "I made it clear why I was here and that I would do anything to find her." He wouldn't bully me into running. I planted my feet shoulder-width apart, ready to fight.

Sterlyn stepped into the back, her eyes tense. "What were you thinking, coming in here acting like that?" she hissed, not quite too low for me to hear.

"What were *you* thinking," he parroted back, spinning to face her with a sneer, "bringing her here? You know today isn't a visitation day."

They were *really* hung up on that. Was the entire campus part of a secret society? Maybe that was why this place gave me the jitters. My mere presence bothered everyone.

"If I hadn't brought her here, where do you think she would have gone?" Sterlyn crossed her arms and shifted her weight to one side. "You obviously wanted her protected last night—that's why you brought her to me—and that's exactly what I'm doing."

"You and Veronica here are missing the point," he said, lifting his hands in my direction. "She was supposed to leave, not stay. Had she left, there wouldn't be problems added to what we already have."

Oh, hell no. I hated being mocked. I placed my hands on my hips and cleared my throat to get their attention. "Sterlyn understands me. You're the one who's slow." I lifted my chin, wanting him to see how serious I was. "I'm *not* leaving without Annie. I'm not sure how many times I have to say that for you to understand, but I've told you more than half a dozen times. That's why I checked into the hotel."

He exhaled and ran his fingers through his hair. "Do you not have any sense of self-preservation?"

"Why do you care?" He didn't have anything invested in my situation, other than being down one favor.

So what if something happened to me? He wouldn't lose sleep over it. "You just met me last night, so it'd be a whole lot easier if you walked away." My chest constricted, becoming too small for my heart. I needed him to be the one to do it. The more he came around, the more I didn't want him to go, but that petrified me. We were from two different worlds. I would only get hurt if we continued to interact.

"I ..." He ran a hand down his face.

Sterlyn arched an eyebrow, and he stiffened again.

"I stuck my neck out for you twice." He glared at me

and pointed at his neck in emphasis. "If I hadn't been there, no telling what state you'd be in."

His words hit my stomach hard. He was right. Klyn had intended to hurt me at the bar, and then whoever had tried to get into my hotel room ... Hell, I should ask Alex who it was again. I never got an answer last time. Regardless, those were two separate events. Still, it didn't change anything. "And I appreciate that." I let the sincerity flow into my tone. I wanted to say more, but my throat dried up, the first sign that I might cry. I wanted to push harder for answers, but then the waterworks would be a given. I couldn't risk them seeing me as weak.

"Don't be so hard on her," Sterlyn chastised and strolled over to me. She placed a hand on my shoulder, glaring at Alex, and my blood revved again. "Imagine if Gwen or Matthew were in trouble. Would you just walk away?"

He shrugged and pursed his lips. "Probably. They can take care of themselves."

Wow. "You'd leave your family hanging?" My cheeks warmed as I remembered how much hell I'd given him over his sister, but in my defense, I had thought they were lovers, which had made the entire situation worse. I pushed the embarrassment aside. "Who does that?"

"I'd do the same thing if I were in her shoes." Sterlyn moved next to me. "So back off. If you don't want her to get hurt, *you* should help her instead."

Alex wrinkled his nose. "How am I supposed to do that, given the situation?"

"What situation?" Did they both consider me looking for Annie a problem? "Annie came to visit someone in *your* town and has gone missing."

"How do you know it's my town?" His mouth dropped for a second before he shut it and glared at Sterlyn. "And yes, that situation. The university doesn't approve of students dating people who aren't—" He stopped, his lips smooshing together.

This had to be a sick joke. "Are you saying students can't date anyone who doesn't go here?" Was that even legal? They already had three younger individuals on the town council—which, now that I thought about it, was odd —and now this.

"Yes." Alex nodded way too hard. "That's exactly what I mean."

This was complete bullshit. This place got worse by the second. "Whatever. No one should help me if they don't want to." I wanted to get away. I hadn't been involved in such a contentious confrontation since the night the shadow had tried to kill me. Despite it being over five years ago, I remembered the image vividly, the dark hand reaching for me. I'd known something sinister had been brewing underneath. The home had wanted to lock me up that night, but Eliza had learned about me and offered to take me in. They'd been so relieved not to have to deal with me anymore. "I'll go to the admissions office and find out where her boyfriend lives."

"Do you know his name?" Alex sounded defeated, which was funny. "And do you expect them to tell you anything? All you'll do is draw more attention, which you're clearly good at."

My hands clenched, and I desperately wanted to punch him. Or kiss him to shut him up. Maybe both.

Something was wrong with me. I should have been appalled and filled with disgust. "No, I don't know his name." I chose to ignore the rest of his statement. "But I know he gave Annie a tour, and since I know *her name,* they should be able to help me." Hopefully, the people in the admissions office were more grounded than the asshat in front of me.

"He was her tour guide?" He squinted and his lip curled with disgust. "I thought ..." His focus cut to Sterlyn.

She lifted a hand. "Me, too. I don't know what happened."

"You thought what?" Clearly, they didn't like this news, but I didn't understand why. They were keeping yet another thing from me. I could only think of one objection to Annie's now-boyfriend giving her the tour. "Is it because it was a guy?" Maybe only same-gendered people gave the tours?

"Something like that." Sterlyn smiled. "But you're right. They should be able to find out who it was."

"You stay here and work." Alex rolled his shoulders. "Let me do some digging, and we can go from there."

"Digging?" If he thought he'd be leaving me in the dark, I'd teach him otherwise. "What does that mean? I have two legs and can get myself to the admissions office. It's literally right around the corner."

"Just ... please." All the animosity left him, and he gave me a half-hearted grin. "Let me go. You aren't supposed to be on campus, and they might not talk to you. I'll figure it out if you promise to stay back here."

"How do I know you'll do it? I want to find her as soon as possible—it could be faster if I went myself." Although, the thought of heading out there with everyone staring at me caused me to shiver. If I didn't know any better, I'd think they wanted to eat me alive, and I'd had some horrible looks thrown my way before.

"Oh, don't worry." He stepped toward the door. "I don't want you here any longer than you have to be."

His words stung. I felt the same way about him, but

hearing it aloud burned. That was a good thing, though. It reminded me he didn't like me. That I was merely a nuisance. He just had misguided concern for my well-being because he'd already saved me twice. I couldn't blame him for wanting me gone so he could go back to living his life without worrying about a girl causing problems. "Fine."

"Good." He nodded and strolled to the door before stopping. "What's her name?"

It took a second for the question to filter through because I'd been watching his ass. "Annie Williams."

"Got it." He strolled away without a backward glance.

Just like last night, a piece of me left along with him, and my heart ached.

As the door closed behind him, I heard Carter ask, "Did you straighten all that out?"

Silence was Alex's response. The guy could be an asshole.

Sterlyn's hand dropped. "Hey, are you okay?" Concern laced each word, and I forced myself not to react negatively.

"Yeah." I spun back around and snatched a towel to wipe down the food preparation area. I'd been cleaning as I went, so the counter didn't need it, but I wanted to avoid looking at her. "Why wouldn't I be?"

"Alex can be a handful," she said softly. "And he's acting over the top, even for him, but I'm glad he's invested in you. You're a good person."

"How can you be so sure?" The bleak thoughts that used to plague me had infiltrated my dreams last night. Not like they used to, but I'd held them at bay for so long that it had caught me off guard. I'd pushed them from my brain this morning, hoping they'd only come back because I was away from home and worried about Annie.

She moved her head and stared at me until I couldn't avoid her gaze and whispered, "Because I know."

"But you might be wrong." The words tumbled out on their own. Growing up, I'd thought I was meant for the shadows, and now that fear had taken root inside me once more.

"I know things." She tapped her head and smiled. "Trust me."

I wanted to, but something inside me cried that she was wrong.

"Sterlyn!" Carter called. "Get out here, please. People are growing impatient."

She rolled her eyes. "All right. Duty calls. Are you good here by yourself?"

"Yup." That was how I preferred it. Sometimes, even being around Eliza and Annie was too much for me and I needed to hide in my room to reset. And with the new craziness simmering inside me, I didn't want to talk or discuss anything else. I wanted to lose myself in the work. "Thanks, though."

After she'd left, I inhaled deeply. Everything would be okay. I'd get out of here today, with Annie. Surely. I'd go back to my life and forget all about Alex and Sterlyn.

The thought of forgetting Sterlyn was about as upsetting as the thought of forgetting Alex. I'd already let too many people in. That was how I'd gotten into this mess to begin with.

I got back to work and tried not to stare at the clock.

BY TEN, the morning rush had calmed down, which wasn't a good thing. I was well aware that Alex still hadn't returned.

I stepped out of the kitchen and found a handsome man standing next to Griffin on the other side of the counter from Sterlyn. The guy was a few inches shorter than Griffin and had dark cappuccino-brown hair styled in spikes. His warm dark-chocolate brown eyes focused on me as his brows furrowed. He nodded, and Sterlyn turned around.

She exhaled. "Is everything okay?"

Two girls sitting at a nearby table turned to us. Their eyes locked on me, but unlike the hateful expressions I'd gotten from others, they just appeared curious.

Now I felt like I was some sort of attraction. I'd take the glares over this any day. "I wanted to get out of the kitchen and see if you'd heard from Alex."

"Ahh ... Alex." The new guy looked at Griffin, and something strange crossed his face. "I still can't get over that."

"Me neither." Griffin huffed. "Veronica, head back to the kitchen."

Oh, hell no. He didn't get to talk to me that way. Authority and I didn't go hand in hand. It was easier listening to Eliza, Annie, and Sterlyn because I felt as if they cared.

Sterlyn.

Dammit.

She'd weaseled her way in.

I stayed put, refusing to budge.

"Another stubborn woman." The guy chuckled and held his hand out to me. "I'm Killian."

He was being nice, so I pushed aside the urge to ignore him

and took his outstretched hand. Our skin touched, and warmth poured off him, turning my palm clammy. I pulled my hand away. "Are you feeling okay?" He had to be running a fever.

"What?" He stared at me and tilted his head. "Not bad at all. Why would you ask?"

I'd reached for his hand again when a low hiss filled the coffee shop. Alex bit out, "Do *not* touch him."

So, of course, I did the only thing I could do—I ignored him and grabbed Killian's hand.

CHAPTER NINE

As soon as my hand touched Killian's again, the warmth damn near burned me. With the fever he had to be running, I couldn't fathom how he was standing here, appearing normal and put together. If it were me, I'd be sweaty, clammy, and flushed.

Definitely flushed.

He cleared his throat and removed his hand from mine, giving Sterlyn and Griffin a sideways glance.

A low growl rattled Alex's chest as he marched over and stopped next to Killian, his attention on me.

What the hell was his problem? And why did his reaction thrill me? Not only did he know I was worried about Annie, but he was nearly losing it because I was touching Killian out of concern.

I pursed my lips, not letting Alex distract me from my mission. I dropped my hand and said, "You're so warm that you have to be feverish. You should be in bed."

Killian nodded at Sterlyn as if they were having a silent conversation and picked up his cup of coffee from the counter.

So Sterlyn was close enough to two guys that she could communicate nonverbally with them. That seemed strange, but Griffin didn't appear fazed by it. Maybe they had a polyamorous relationship. They were equally hot, so I wouldn't blame her. Although Killian hadn't been at the house last night.

He took a sip and then held the cup toward me. "I'm sure the warmth from my coffee isn't helping matters."

Of course. He'd been cradling a cup of coffee. No wonder his hands were so warm.

Whatever. I was losing it.

"Why are you out here?" Alex spoke through gritted teeth.

I faced him and instantly regretted it. His intense gaze stripped me—like he could see right inside my soul. The more I was around him, the more desperate I was for him to never leave, which was dangerous. If I felt like this after a day, I didn't need to stay any longer.

But if I stayed, he'd keep showing up. Inherently, I knew this, and it concerned me how damn thrilled it made me.

I came close to averting my gaze, but that would reveal he had some dominance over me. I was determined to hide that instinct to submit. "Because I wanted a break. Not that I owe you an explanation."

"You don't owe me?" He laughed charmingly and winked, his flirty disposition slipping back into place. "Oh, you do, but I won't be cashing it in for an explanation." The sexual innuendo was like a neon sign as he perused my body.

And my damn traitorous body responded. The image of his mouth on mine and his hands all over me had me breathing harder.

He smirked as if aware of what was going on inside me. "If you're up for it now ..."

"No, she's not." Sterlyn clutched my arm and dragged me closer to her side. "She's not going anywhere alone with you." Her protective tone further rattled my defenses.

Dammit. This sealed a friendship between us. People with my best interests at heart prevented me from making horrible mistakes. And doing anything with Alex would only shatter me. "Yeah, what she said." My voice was breathless, but the words came out somewhat strong.

"Then I guess I can't share with you what I learned." Alex shrugged and waggled his eyebrows. "That suits me just fine. You can head home before causing any more trouble."

"What?" My breath caught. He *had* found something out. Thank God. Without thinking, I took a few steps toward the counter, closer to him. "Is she okay?"

"Let's talk out back." He glanced over his shoulder as a group of people, with Gwen in the center, stopped in their tracks and stared at us. A vein bulged in his neck as he pivoted, walking around Killian and Griffin and behind the counter. "Gwen is supposed to be in class, but she's over here snooping instead."

"What the hell?" Carter turned off the milk steamer and dropped his head. "I swear it's like I have no authority here despite being the manager."

"Maybe if you alpha up, others wouldn't mind listening," Alex snapped and brushed past the poor guy, heading toward the kitchen.

Wow. That wasn't very nice, so I gave Carter a sad smile and said, "I'm sorry about him, but I do appreciate you letting me help out today."

"Oh, you know." He put his hands in the pocket of his

jeans. "It was nothing." His cheeks turned pink as if he wasn't used to the attention.

Not wanting Alex to leave before I had a chance to hear what he'd discovered, I rushed into the kitchen and found him leaning against the counter with his arms crossed. His body shook with rage as he waited.

"Well?" I wanted to know everything. Every single last detail he'd learned.

But he ignored me as he kept his sights on the door.

Nope, that wasn't how this worked. "What did you find out?" I asked more loudly, placing my body in his line of sight.

"I heard you," he gritted out.

I bit my tongue, waiting for him to continue, but he remained silent. "Oh, well, you can understand my confusion, seeing as you aren't talking." I wanted to smack him and kiss him all at the same time. The weird mix of emotions built in my chest and prickled over my skin like electricity, ripping me in two.

Sterlyn joined us, hands raised. "Look, I didn't know she was going to walk out front."

What was *up* with them hiding me back here? Why the hell did they care? "What's the big deal?" I was done going with the flow. I needed to figure this all out if I wanted to get Annie out of this. What the hell had she gotten us mixed up with? "So what if I went out front? Am I not bougie enough to be seen here?"

"Bougie?" Alex's forehead lined. "What does that mean?"

"Classy?" That was the nice way of putting it, so of course, I couldn't stop there. "Pompous? Gaudy?"

"Tell us what you really think." Sterlyn chuckled and placed an arm around my shoulders.

I calmed at her touch, and my eyes widened. "Should I keep going?" Bantering with her felt natural.

"No, we're good." Alex frowned and exhaled then jumped right into what I wanted to hear. "The person who was supposed to give your sister a school tour disappeared that day."

"What do you mean, *disappeared?*" That didn't sound good. "Is she okay?"

"Yeah, she's fine." He straightened from the counter and ran a hand down his neck. "I had to find her. That's what took so long. Anyway, we can talk about that later." He gestured to Sterlyn. "But I found out who did give Annie the tour, and I know exactly where they are."

"Really?" This felt too easy, but that was probably because he was the one who'd gotten the information. If it had been me, I wouldn't have known where to find the person. "Okay, let's go."

"I'll go alone." Alex sighed. "I was just giving you an update as promised."

"Oh, hell no." Yeah, he might be helping me, but I had to get Annie. She would be uncomfortable with him. At least, I hoped she'd refuse to leave with him because she didn't know him. "I'm going too. I have to see her." I wasn't above begging him. "Please."

He shook his head. "No. It's safer for you here than at the bar."

"She's at Thirsty's?" That confirmed my worst fears. Annie was in over her head and putting herself at risk, leaving Eliza and me at home, worried sick about her.

"Yes." Alex leaned toward me. His sweet scent swirled through the room, and I found myself leaning toward him, too. "And you know how that went last night. I'll bring her to Sterlyn's." He spun on his heels and marched to the back door. As he took the handle, he paused. "And make sure when you all leave, you go out the back door. Gwen saw you, and she's probably made some calls by now. I won't be there to intercept anyone."

Sterlyn nodded. "Okay."

He strolled out, letting the door slam behind him, and the noise echoed around the kitchen. I'd taken two steps after him before I realized everything in me was urging me to follow him.

Dammit. I had to figure out how to get back to the house and get my car. I didn't want to fight about going to Thirsty's with him because he'd make sure I couldn't go, but there was no way in hell I wasn't showing up there.

"He's right. We need to leave." Sterlyn hurried toward the back door just as the swinging doors opened and Griffin and Killian joined us.

"I don't understand what's going on." I felt even more lost. "What did he intercept, and why the hell is it a big deal?"

"The university doesn't like unvetted visitors." Sterlyn waved for me to follow. "Alex smoothed things over when he went searching for Annie at the office."

I wasn't sure if that made sense, but I needed to find her.

Killian pointed at my apron and held out his hand. "Here, I'll take that and help Carter while the three of you get out of here."

"Wait. How did you know we needed to leave?" Alex hadn't been loud. There was no way Griffin and Killian could've heard him out there, but they'd come back here right as Sterlyn was going to get them.

"A good guess." Killian smiled. "When Alex is involved, things often have to be addressed immediately."

Maybe. Lucky for them, I didn't want to push it. I needed to go. Fortunately, I'd brought my keys with me, so I wouldn't have to waste time going inside Sterlyn and Griffin's house to get them. That would also help prevent them from attempting to talk me out of going to Thirsty's. I'd jump out of their car and run to mine.

"Thanks, Kill," Sterlyn said softly as she removed her apron. "I'll be back soon, but I feel like Griffin and I need to stay with her."

"You do." He rubbed his hands together and smirked. "It'll be fun working with Carter. We got this."

"Fun?" Griffin snorted. "Sure, go with that. He'll still tell you what to do, despite you being his al ... leader."

"You're his leader?" What did that even mean? They were a bunch of college kids. "In a fraternity or something?" I could see Killian being the president of some fraternity or something. He had the looks and charming personality.

Killian put the apron on and tied it in the back. "Something like that."

I'd expected him to appear silly, but he pulled off the apron. Every person I'd run into here at Shadow Ridge and Shadow Terrace was gorgeous. Not even one person could be considered average.

"Let's get out of here." Griffin walked to the back door and opened it, his face twisting in disgust.

Not sure what was going on, I rushed toward him, but something rotten filled my nose. "Holy shit. Did someone die back here?" I dry-heaved from the stench, and my eyes watered.

"It's just the dumpster." Sterlyn rushed past me and out the door. She moved quickly, and for the first time, I'd found someone who ran at the same speed as me.

Usually, I was faster than everybody. Back in school,

during the track and field unit in gym class, I'd been accused of taking steroids.

Following Sterlyn and Griffin, I passed the dumpster and hurried toward the vehicle. The air cleared as we got closer to the Navigator, and I caught up to them at the car. I glanced at Sterlyn to find her watching me, her head tilted.

"What?" I rubbed my face, wondering if I had something on it.

"You're ... fast," she said slowly. "Have you always been able to run like that?"

"Uh ... yeah." I looked back at her and raised a brow. She'd run as fast as me. It shouldn't have been a huge deal, but her eyes were alight with curiosity.

That was never a good sign.

The locks clicked, informing me that Griffin had unlocked the car, and I climbed in, avoiding Sterlyn's uncomfortable attention. Sitting behind her would make it harder for her to focus on me.

Griffin and Sterlyn got into the car, and we pulled out of the university, heading toward their home. I kept waiting for Sterlyn to talk again, but she remained quiet the entire way there.

When we pulled into the garage at their house, I jumped out of the vehicle and charged toward my car.

"You'll be careful, right?" Sterlyn asked, and I turned to glimpse back at her. She'd gotten out but still had her hand on the car door.

I wasn't sure how to respond. I'd expected her to demand I come into the house, not essentially give me her blessing to take off.

"You're going to the bar, right?" Sterlyn pointed at the car keys in my hand.

Scowling, Griffin walked around the car. "You need to stay with us."

"I *can't*." They had to understand. "I appreciate everything you've done for me, but Annie doesn't know Alex. I need to be there to bring her home. Not him."

"Look—" Griffin started, but Sterlyn cut him off.

"If it was Killian, what would you do if you were in her shoes?" Sterlyn sighed, concern etched on her face. "You'd do whatever it took to get him home. You wouldn't trust Alex. Can you really blame her?"

"No, but—"

This time, I interrupted him. "I'm not asking for your permission." What was it with these people ordering me around?

I turned back around and continued marching toward my car, not bothering to glance back, but then something cold grabbed my arm.

A chill ran through my body. Sterlyn and Griffin hadn't been close enough to catch me. So who was here?

CHAPTER TEN

I spun, ready to fight. When Sterlyn's face came into view, my breath whooshed out, and my heart returned to a normal rhythm. I'd expected the guy who'd attacked me last night or worse ... Alex.

Something hardened in my chest. I hadn't been that far from Sterlyn, but she couldn't have reached me that fast. At the bare minimum, I should've heard her footsteps behind me.

She dropped her hand and stepped back like she realized she'd done something wrong. "Before you go, make sure you have my number."

"What?" My mind struggled to catch up to what she'd said. I couldn't help fixating on how fast she'd reached me. "Why?"

"In case something happens, and you need me." She shrugged nonchalantly, but her face was lined with worry.

There was something she wasn't telling me.

Shocker.

"Yeah, okay." I held my hand out for her phone. "I'll plug my number into yours."

She nodded and placed her phone in my hand. "Please. And don't hesitate to call us if you need anything."

I should have left it at that, but I couldn't. "How'd you reach me so fast?" I pulled up a text and typed in my number, doing my best not to make her feel defensive. I wanted the truth.

"Oh, that." She forced out a laugh. "I've run daily my entire life."

"Right," I said like I believed her. Maybe she was fast from daily training, but she'd moved at blinding speed with no sign of exertion.

I sighed and handed her back her phone. I needed to find Annie, so she wasn't left too long with Alex. "There you go. Text me, and I'll save you as a contact." I unlocked the car door and climbed in, itching to get moving.

Alex was unpredictable at best, and I didn't want him to intimidate Annie.

"Be careful, and keep an eye on your surroundings," Sterlyn said and shut the door. She took a few steps back and watched me pull out of the driveway.

Under normal circumstances, I wouldn't have run off like this. I'd be more cautious, like Sterlyn, but Annie was wary of strangers like me.

I followed the main road to the two-way lane that led to Shadow Terrace. Once again, the road was deserted. For a bustling town that tourists frequented, I'd have thought there would be at least a few cars.

The road went on for miles. Just like the night before, I almost wondered if I'd taken a wrong turn. The creepy feeling didn't hit me, but I wasn't sure if that was a good thing, seeing as it had never really left. But that was something to ponder on another day.

Finally, the town appeared, and it looked even more

gorgeous in the sunlight. The white paint sparkled invit-
ingly, and I could see the clocktower from here. As I pulled
onto the cobblestone streets, I noticed more people were
milling around. A few groups of families walked down the
street, pointing at the buildings and a sizable water fountain
in the center of a circle. Everything seemed normal, unlike
last night.

As I neared the bar, I passed a couple dressed all in
black and standing in the shadows of the shop awnings.
Their universally pasty white skin again reminded me of
the grim reaper.

A warning sensation tickled the back of my neck as the
coolness of the shadow surrounded me. Was I imagining it
again?

None of the other passersby noticed the odd couple. I
wanted to yell and scream *run*, but all that would do was
draw attention to me. Besides, the two ghostly people
weren't paying attention to anyone else either, focusing
more on staying hidden in shady spots.

Thirsty's came into view, and my heart rate picked up.
Annie might be inside with her weird new boyfriend, the
one she shouldn't have even met. The expression on Alex's
face when he'd said that her tour guide had disappeared had
unnerved me.

More cars were parked on the street today, making the
place seem less threatening. I parallel parked a block away
from the bar and turned off my car. I scanned the area for
anything strange, but the place was filled with normal-
looking people going about their day.

Where had they all been last night?

I climbed out of the car and locked the door then
headed across the street to the bar. Klyn popped into my
head, and I stumbled, the memory of him pushing me

against the wall to attack me replaying in my mind. Surely, he wouldn't be here now. Besides, everything else had a normal feel. Maybe my imagination had gotten the better of me last night, and his actions hadn't been as threatening as I remembered?

Before I could second-guess anything else, I pushed open the door and stepped inside the bar. It was just as dark as last night and somehow smelled like a bakery. I blinked to adjust my eyes to the dimness then shivered as Alex's voice filled my ears.

"This is unacceptable." His voice was low and cold. "We've talked about this."

The room came into focus, and I saw Alex leaning over a booth, his hands clenched into fists.

Annie's trademark red lipstick and long, wavy, brown-sugar-colored hair caught my attention from the recesses of the booth. She had her head on the shoulder of a handsome but sinister-appearing man. His ivory skin was nearly as pale as the couple's in black had been, and his jet-black hair rivaled Annie's in length. But the creepiest part was his ice-blue eyes.

She usually went for sun-kissed athletic guys, so to see her all over this guy convinced me that something was seriously wrong.

"Annie!" I called and hurried toward them.

Alex whipped his head around and glared at me but surprisingly remained silent.

Annie didn't bother to look at me, keeping her head on the guy's shoulder as she ran her fingertips along his black shirt sleeve.

What the hell? This would be harder than I'd feared. Ignoring the stares—at this point, I was used to them—I planted myself next to Alex. "*Annie*," I said even louder.

Alex tensed and went as still as a statue, but that was his own damn fault. He should've known better than to come here without me. I ran my gaze over my sister and went still enough to rival Alex as something sickening caught my attention.

She had bite marks on her neck. Not just one but three from what I could see.

Oh, *hell* no. "It's time to go."

But Annie just sat there, ignoring me, her attention on the man beside her. It was as if she couldn't see or hear anyone but him.

"Who are you?" the man cooed, scanning me from head to toe.

She didn't even seem to notice, just scooted closer to him. The neckline of her blue sundress slipped lower as she leaned over to get him to focus back on her. "Baby." She grabbed the side of his face, forcing him to glance down at her breasts. "You know I want all the attention."

He chuckled sinisterly. "And you have most of my attention, but I've told you I love to sample others, too. Don't worry. You're my main girl."

A giggle was her response. A fucking *giggle*.

She'd lost her damn mind. I stepped around Alex, took Annie by the arm, and whispered, "We're going home." I couldn't let her stay here another second longer, making a complete ass out of herself. The only explanation I could come up with was that an alien had invaded her body.

"Who the hell are you?" She tried to yank her arm from my grasp as her head snapped in my direction. Her espresso-colored eyes filled with confusion. "Leave me alone!"

Her words slapped me in the face. After all we'd gone through together, *this* was how she treated me? "Who the hell am I?" My voice grew louder. I was causing a scene, but I didn't give a damn. My best friend—my sister—was pretending not to know me. "Do you find this funny?"

"Veronica." Alex's voice was a warning, but I didn't care.

I reached for her again, and she scooted closer to the douchebag. She whimpered and nuzzled into his side. "Save me. This freak is going to hurt me."

"He's the one hurting you!" I gestured to her neck. "You're letting him *bite* you. God, Annie. What has he done to you?"

"I've allowed her to be free." The guy smirked and wrapped his arm tighter around my best friend. "To release her worries and doubts and to live life to the fullest."

"Eilam," Alex rasped. "You need to stop this. *Now.*"

"Or what?" Eilam lifted a brow and leaned back in his seat as he gazed at Alex. He chuckled. "Are you pretending you're actually going to do something about it? It's not like I'm your only issue." He waved a hand. "Look around."

I sucked in a breath as I realized Klyn was here. A few other men were also inching closer to us. They were paying close attention to me. The warning tickle on the back of my neck went off again. I had to get out of here.

Correction—Annie and I had to get out of here.

"Please, Annie," I groveled, desperate to get her to leave with me. "Eliza is worried. We need to get home."

"Eliza?" Her brows furrowed. "Who is that?"

I gasped. She wasn't playing a game. She truly didn't remember who Eliza and I were. How the hell was that possible?

"She's feisty." A tall, slender guy stepped closer to me. "I can only imagine how she'd be in bed."

Ew. No. Definitely. Not. Happening. "Come on, Annie. We have to *go*."

"How does she know my name?" Annie asked as she scooted into the guy's lap to get farther away from me. "Who is that, Eilam?"

As I leaned over to yank her from her seat, Alex wrapped an arm around me and pulled me against his chest.

Tingles sparked between us, and a low moan escaped me. Before I could even register his intention, his soft, firm lips landed on mine.

The asshole was kissing me! Something was wrong with every single person here. I pushed against his chest to get out of his hold, but his mouth continued to seduce mine. My lips prickled and parted of their own accord as whatever was between us grew stronger.

His tongue darted from his mouth and tasted my lips, and the kiss took on a life of its own. His rich bourbon taste filled me, and the world around me became hazy. I was supposed to be doing something important, but I couldn't bring it to the forefront of my mind.

Alex pulled me closer, his arms wrapping around my body and his hands settling on my ass. I opened my mouth, completely at his mercy. His tongue pressed inside, stroking me. Between the feel of him and his sweet taste, I couldn't get enough.

I'd never been kissed like this, and God knew I never would be again. My arms wrapped around his neck, and my fingers fisted in his hair. Every ounce of self-control I'd learned over nearly twenty years dissolved from just a taste of him.

A low groan escaped the back of his throat as his fingers kneaded my ass, turning me on in ways I'd never thought possible. My body warmed, and a deep ache pulsed inside me.

His teeth raked my lip, and a metallic taste filled my mouth. Instead of bringing pain, it increased the pressure, and the connection between us solidified even more. I didn't understand what was going on, but I didn't want this to stop.

Kissing him forever would never be enough; I jumped up and wrapped my legs around his waist.

He stumbled back, pressing my breasts to him as a guttural moan shook his chest. I should've been worried that he'd fall or drop me, but something inside me knew he'd never allow anything bad to happen to me. He sat down suddenly, allowing me to straddle him. His hardness rubbed against my core.

All I could think about was getting him inside me, and I ground against him as I took control. Only the two of us existed in the world, and our connection urged us closer. I'd never felt such an overpowering need before, and the way his arms grasped my body told me he felt the same.

Something hovered over us. A presence I couldn't shake, no matter how hard I tried. It pulled me out of the moment as reality settled back around me. Holy shit, what was I doing?

I pushed against Alex's chest, trying to come up for air, but his hand cupped the back of my neck, deepening the kiss. It would have been so easy to fall back into the moment with him. Making myself pull away from him upset me.

In other words, I'd let this go too far.

I have to save Annie.

Someone beside me hissed, "What the fuck do you think you're doing, Alex?"

Alex pulled back abruptly and shook his head no.

I turned to the right to see a man with two long, sharp, pointed fangs protruding from his mouth. His eyes burned crimson.

A scream caught in my throat as I came face to face with a vampire.

CHAPTER ELEVEN

My heart pounded in my ears as I stared at the most terrifying thing I'd ever seen.

Flashes of Annie's bite marks popped into my mind. The douchebag was a vampire too! And Klyn had been going for my neck.

Nausea washed over me, and I pressed closer to Alex. Something cold formed in my chest.

Alex had known what was going on the entire time.

"What are you doing, *Brother?*" the scary vampire asked Alex.

Could that mean...?

No.

"Matthew, please calm down," Alex said. He slid me off his lap and stood, stepping slightly in front of me, blocking me from the vampire's view. "It's not what it looks like."

"You didn't just claim a human in front of everyone?" the vampire hissed.

"Human?" I squeaked, still processing everything.

This had to be a nightmare. It was the only damn thing

that made any sense. Vampires weren't real. Supernaturals didn't exist.

I stood beside Alex, needing to make sure the fangs and red eyes weren't part of my imagination.

But no, if anything, the fangs were longer ... sharper. And his irises were the color of blood.

Matthew chuckled darkly. "It's so cute you think Alex is safer than me."

"Shut up," Alex half bellowed. "I am not a threat to her."

"She's a human." Matthew licked his lips as he stared at my neck. "We're all a threat to her, especially once we get a taste."

"Do not come near her." Alex fisted his hands. "I won't let anyone hurt her."

His own fangs descended.

My heart stopped. It had been one thing to assume he was a vampire; it was a whole different thing to see it. I looked back at Annie, who was now straddling the douchebag. His teeth sank into her neck, and he drank again. She writhed against him in ecstasy as blood trickled down the corners of his mouth.

This was all too much. The urge to flee sank deep, but the world tilted, preventing me from rushing to the door. I wobbled onto my feet as panic closed its iron grasp around me.

"Dammit, Matthew," Alex growled.

A strong arm wrapped around my waist, and another slid underneath my knees. I was picked up and cradled against a hard, cool chest that smelled uniquely of Alex. Panic clawed inside me, yet part of me was comforted. The two parts fought each other, but it didn't matter which side won out because I was frozen in place by fear.

"Do not walk away from me," Matthew called after us.

Alex didn't even slow down. His back hit something, and daylight flooded my eyes. I clamped them shut at the stark change in lighting.

"I told you to stay with Sterlyn," Alex complained under his breath. "Now I bet you wish you'd listened to me."

The sad truth was I did. But that wouldn't have solved a damn thing. My sister didn't remember me, and she was letting some sick, sadistic vampire *feed* off her.

Oh God, I was going to be sick. The image of his mouth on her neck made me woozier.

A car door opened, and Alex gently sat me down on the passenger seat of a luxury SUV. A Mercedes emblem was discreetly displayed on the dashboard, and the car smelled brand new. Between the gadgets, smooth black leather, and the spotlessness, I would bet the car was worth more than I made in three years.

Within seconds, Alex had climbed into the driver's side, and we were out of the parking spot before I even realized the car was on.

I wanted to scream, cry, curse, and jump out of the car, but I sat frozen, unmoving except for the steady rise and fall of my chest.

I focused all my energy on breathing. I'd been like this once before, the night I'd thought the shadow had attacked me. The counselor had muttered about anxiety attacks and mental breakdowns over and over. Once I'd been able to speak again and told them my story, they'd written *mental breakdown* into my record, intending to send me to a psych ward.

Sometimes, I thought I was truly disturbed and had

imagined that night, as well as today. But those memories felt too vivid to be a figment of my imagination.

"I'm sorry, Veronica." Alex huffed as he turned the vehicle onto the main road out of town. "I didn't mean for any of this to happen. I tried to get you to leave. I didn't want this for you." He placed a hand on my leg.

No matter how nice it felt, I couldn't stop picturing him with fangs. I jerked toward the door, finally able to move. His hand fell to the side and hurt flashed across his face.

"You're a ... vampire?" My words sounded breathless.

He rubbed a hand down his face as he kept one hand on the steering wheel. "Would you even believe me if I said no?"

That was such a strange thing to say, but he got his point across. "No, you're right. I saw you. Your teeth." Shit! He'd bitten my lip. I touched where he'd bitten me, only to find my skin unmarred. "How?"

"I was born this way," he said, answering the question he thought I was asking.

"No, you bit my lip." I pulled the visor down and flipped its mirror open. I examined my lips, but nothing seemed out of the ordinary, except they were more swollen and pinker from our kiss. "But there isn't a mark." Dark circles lined my eyes, emphasizing their emerald irises and the red in my hair.

"That's because my saliva healed it." He looked at me with a frown. "I'm sorry. I didn't mean to bite you. I lost my head for a second. I hope it didn't hurt."

"Am I going to turn?" That was what happened in movies and books.

He shook his head. "No, I didn't inject you with venom."

This was the craziest conversation I'd ever had, which was saying something.

He'd bitten me.

And I'd *liked* it.

What the hell did that say about me? Probably things I didn't want to analyze.

My mind raced, but I couldn't comprehend anything, so my mouth blurted, "What do you mean you were born?"

"Just that. Vampires can produce offspring, and no one in my family has been turned, so I have authentic, undiluted vampire blood running through my veins."

The more he talked, the less anything made sense. "But you don't change, so how is that possible?"

"We're born infants just like humans, but once we reach our twenties, we stop maturing." His knee bopped, the only sign he was uncomfortable with this conversation.

"Do you only eat blood?" Questions spilled from my lips. "And do you turn into a bat?" That last part varied greatly depending on the movie or story.

He chuckled, his voice devoid of humor. "Yes, vampires need blood to survive. We can eat food, but it's not enjoyable." He exhaled. "And no, we don't change into bats. We have super speed, supernatural strength, and the ability to go long periods of time without eating, but we still need sustenance and oxygen."

My heart hammered in my chest as my anxiety picked back up. Blackness hazed the edges of my vision. If I didn't get myself together, I'd pass out.

I was alone in a car with a self-proclaimed vampire.

That couldn't be safe. I inhaled deeply to get oxygen to my brain, but hysteria attempted to filter back in.

"Veronica." The sound of my name on his lips reminded me of a song. "I really am sorry. If I—"

"Please stop." I couldn't take more right now, and whatever chemistry we had was messing with my mind. "I just need quiet."

He nodded, respecting my wishes, which caught me off guard. He normally tried charming his way out of things, but he looked as broken as me. It didn't make sense. His world hadn't been ripped apart. His core beliefs hadn't been shaken.

I wrapped my arms around myself, trying to warm up again. I felt so cold inside, like something was calling out to me, whispering promises of retribution or revenge, but the problem was I didn't want that.

At least, not with Alex. But why? He was a predator, and I was his prey. Being this close to him was a risk ... but staying away from him might break me.

The farther away I got from Annie, the more time my mind had to catch up with everything.

That guy had been feeding off her when we'd left, and I hadn't put up a fight. What kind of sister *did* that? "We need to go back."

"What?" He glanced at me before refocusing on the road. "No. That's not happening."

"That guy was feeding off Annie." I sounded insane, but I'd seen it with my own two eyes. "He could kill her!"

Alex shifted in his seat. "He won't."

"Oh, wow." I couldn't believe him. "A vampire trying to reassure me that another of his kind won't hurt someone. How could you possibly know that? You told me that vampires need blood to survive."

"Yes, but he won't hurt her with Matthew there. Our family is the purest bloodline, descended from the first original vampire, who was cursed by a demon, so we're stronger than the others, and Matthew is his king." He cleared his throat and cracked his knuckles. "Matthew thought I was doing the same to you. That's why he almost lost it."

"You bit me." My mind was fogged with all this information. "Remember?" I pointed at my lip and regretted it. My lips still buzzed from his kiss. I was tempted to kiss him to the point of senselessness again, to forget everything I'd seen. But as soon as we stopped, reality would flood back into me.

He scowled. "That was different, and you know it."

"Oh, do I?" My voice went high, hinging on hysteria. "I learned about vampires less than ten minutes ago, and now I'm an expert?"

"Dammit, Veronica." He gripped the steering wheel. "I would never hurt you."

"But you did." He had to see that. This wasn't rocket science. "You hid what was going on with my sister from me."

"I didn't know." He pulled over to the side of the road on the outskirts of the town and turned to me. His eyes darkened to a sapphire blue.

"Maybe." But I couldn't allow myself to drop it. "You had an inkling, though. Didn't you?"

His shoulders sagged, and his head drooped. "Yes, but I wasn't sure. This morning, I planned to find your sister and bring her to you, but you couldn't stay put."

"Oh, I'm sorry I didn't trust a man I met less than twenty-four hours ago!" This wasn't my fault, and I wouldn't let him pretend it was. "I mean, silly me. It's not like I just learned he's a fucking vampire who didn't think to fill me in on *that* little nugget of information."

"Because you're taking the news so well." His nostrils flared. "Imagine how you would've reacted at the bar if you had known your sister was his midnight snack."

I opened the car door and jumped out.

"Veronica, where are you going?" he called after me.

Prick. Like I was going to tell him anything. For once, he could see how it felt to be on the other side.

A low growl echoed around me as he rasped, "Veronica, come back here."

I pulled the phone out of my back pocket while raising my middle finger at him. If he wanted a response, there, he'd gotten one.

Before he could intercept me, I typed out a message to Sterlyn, hoping she could get here real quick. This whole situation was unraveling.

As expected, Alex's door slammed shut. I hit send just as the jackass appeared beside me.

I jerked back. Stupid supernatural quick speed.

"You can't just walk away from me." His face turned pink.

That fascinated me. *Dammit, Ronnie. Focus.* I shook my head to clear the cobwebs as I squared my shoulders and faced him. "Yes, I can. And I will. I survived nineteen years before meeting you, and I've done a swell job."

"A *swell* job," he said mockingly. "Yeah, you came to a vampire town looking for your brainwashed sister. If it hadn't been for me, you'd have ended up exactly where she is."

He had me there, which pissed me off even more. All I could do was get more defiant. "I would've figured something out." Yeah, probably not, but we would never know. "I can be thrifty when I need to be." Yeah, I was pretty sure *thrifty* wasn't the right word there.

He stepped toward me. "Oh, I'm sure you could've found some surefire cost reduction methods to help you out."

"You ..." Embarrassment and hurt rolled throughout me. "... bastard." I understood I was being unreasonable, but I hadn't even had a moment to process this whole new world. A sob threatened at the back of my throat as everything caught up with me. I bit it back, not wanting him to see me fall apart.

Something unreadable passed between us, an emotion that pulled at my heart, but for the life of me, I couldn't figure out why.

"I wish it didn't have to be this way," he whispered as he stroked my cheek with his fingertips. "But I'd be selfish if I didn't protect you. You'll be harmed if you stay here, and I couldn't live with that."

The sweet gesture and words surprised me, and a tear trailed down my cheek.

His mouth crashed onto mine, and instead of fighting it, I opened myself to him immediately. I needed something ... anything to make the world feel right, and he was my anchor.

My tongue swept across his lips, and he groaned in pleasure. He responded in earnest, and everything fell away. It petrified me that he held so much power, but the idea of not being with him scared me more.

This time, he was the one who pulled back. He placed his forehead against mine and stared at me like he was trying to remember my face.

"What's wrong?" Every ounce of anger disappeared as I watched his face crinkle with pain.

"Everything." He locked eyes with me, and the blue of his irises turned bright. "I'll take you to Sterlyn's where you'll wait until I get your car. Once I bring it to you, you will get in the car and drive straight home. You'll tell Eliza you found Annie and that all is well. That she is thirty minutes behind you."

"But ..."

He continued, ignoring my comment. "When you got here last night, you went to a normal bar and didn't find Annie. The bartender told you she came in around lunch close to daily while in town, so you went back to a hotel room, and nothing strange happened. You never met me, and when you went back the next day, Annie was there with her boyfriend, having a huge fight. She agreed to come home, but she needed to get her stuff. You offered to go with her, but she was adamant that she wanted to go alone. She called you thirty minutes into your drive home, telling you she was packing and about to head home."

I'd let this go on way too long. "Have you lost your mind? None of that happened, and I won't lie to my mother." If he thought telling me what he wanted me to remember would be that easy, I wasn't alone in my insanity. "And is that how easy it's going to be to forget me? You'll just pretend we never met?"

He stepped back and squinted. "That's impossible. You should only remember what I just told you."

Pure rage made my blood boil. "Were you trying to mess with my *mind*?"

CHAPTER TWELVE

I'd never been so angry in my entire life. And the fact that Alex wanted me to forget everything broke me.

I'd always refused to be the girl who got too invested in a man. And here I was, not even twenty-four hours into meeting this one, and he'd hurt me worse than anyone ever had. I wasn't only furious at him but also at myself.

No one except me should ever determine my worth or dictate my feelings about myself.

But he had. He'd gone from making me feel desired to unworthy. Why else would he not want me to remember him?

"It's for your own good." He grimaced like he knew that hadn't been the right thing to say.

"How often do you give a girl the most amazing kiss of her life and then erase her memory?" The thought sickened me. Maybe I was just another notch in his belt. Hell, I probably would have been a complete notch if his brother hadn't interrupted us. I'd been ready to give up my virginity to the guy right there in the middle of the bar. Something was seriously messed up with me.

"Most amazing kiss, eh?" He smiled, his cocky arrogance snapping back into place.

Oh, hell no. "It was mediocre at best. I was just being nice." I couldn't believe I'd given the asshole a compliment. He already had a big enough head.

His nose wrinkled, and he stepped away from me as he waved a hand in front of his face.

Great, now he was disgusted with me. He should be. I was a horrible liar, but I couldn't confirm that he'd rocked my world when he was being obnoxious. I had to get the conversation back on track. "No, you don't get to do that and keep secrets from me."

He lifted his hands in pure frustration. "What did you expect? That I'd bare my soul to a woman I'd just met?" He patted his chest, reminding me of Tarzan. "Fine. You want honesty? Here it goes. Your sister has been mind-fucked by a vampire who has lost most of his humanity."

That didn't make me feel better. "Oh, like you were trying to do to me?" He couldn't pretend he was better than that asshole back there.

He sneered, unhappy with my comparison. "It's different. I was doing it to protect you, not to make you my fucking puppet."

"Some would beg to differ." I wished I could take back the words, but they were out there. I wasn't being kind because I wanted to hurt him like he'd hurt me.

He ignored the jab. "Then maybe you wanted me to tell you that I'm three hundred years old but look your age because we're immortal."

Three *hundred*? I could've gone without knowing.

"Or that when I'm around you, I lose my head," he said, leaning in closer. "And that I should've shoved you in the car and driven you all the way home because what I did back there put a target on your back."

If I'd thought my mind had been spinning earlier, I'd been so wrong. Yes, I was aware that Annie and I were in danger, but the magnitude of the situation hadn't fully sunk in until now, and I had a feeling he wasn't done with his rant.

"Did you contact Sterlyn?" Alex rasped, turning toward the two-lane highway that connected Shadow Terrace to Shadow Ridge.

"Huh?" The abrupt change in the conversation threw me. "Yes, I did." There was no point in lying. "Why?"

He laughed but hurt bled through. "Of course, you did."

The purring of an engine caught my attention, and I turned toward the road to see Griffin's black Navigator heading our way. I guessed it made sense that Alex could hear them before me, being supernatural and all.

"Don't you take that tone with me." Now I sounded like Eliza, but I didn't care. "I just found out you're a *vampire* from your vamped-out brother and discovered that my sister doesn't even remember who I am!"

Both the driver and passenger doors opened, and Griffin and Sterlyn climbed from the car. The back doors also opened. They'd brought people with them.

Crap, I had led them right into trouble. I hadn't been thinking clearly when I'd texted her. "Stay back."

I looked over Alex's shoulder at Sterlyn, Griffin, Killian, and a dirty-blond-haired girl.

"What's going on?" Sterlyn asked slowly, glancing between Alex and me.

"You know you aren't supposed to be here," Alex snapped and turned so he could see both them and me. "The bridge is the marker."

"And there's a good reason for it." They deserved to know what they'd walked into. "It's not safe here."

Alex snorted. "You think they don't know that?"

"Dude." Griffin strolled toward us like he was approaching a caged animal. "What are you doing?"

"She wants to know the truth," Alex said and cut his eyes to me. "Right?"

Now I wasn't so sure, but when you were ignorant, you had no idea what you were up against. It was better to face things head-on, or I hoped it was. "Yes."

"Then you should know—"

"Alex, shut the hell up," Griffin growled, his eyes glowing faintly.

I stumbled back as the cold hard truth crashed into me. "Are you guys vampires too?" Had I been surrounded by them the entire time?

"No, we aren't vampires." Sterlyn gave a tight smile. "The four of us... we're wolf shifters."

Right. Maybe this was all an elaborate prank. Annie liked to play pranks. "What else is there? We've got vampires and wolf shifters. What about witches and angels?" I let the sarcasm drip.

"They're real too." The blond girl nodded as her light gray eyes sparkled. "One of our besties is an angel. She'll be at Sterlyn's soon."

"Man, you do realize that it isn't your house anymore?" Killian chuckled and nudged Griffin with his elbow. "It's now Sterlyn's alone."

"That's fine with me." Griffin beamed. "As long as she's right beside me, it can be all hers."

"Oh, gag me." The blond girl cringed. "Just ignore them. They're still new to their relationship."

Killian rolled his eyes. "Like it's getting any better."

"As grateful as I am that the four of you came when Veronica contacted you, your presence is no longer required," Alex said with an air of authority as he stepped in front of me. "You all better go before someone less under-standing finds you in this city."

"Wait. You visited them last night with no issues, but they can't come to see you?" I moved to stand beside him. "How is that fair?"

"Sterlyn, you were right." The blond girl clapped her hands. "I do like her." She marched over to me and held out her hand. "I'm Sierra, and you're Ronnie, right?"

"No, her name is Veronica," Alex corrected as he grabbed my hand before it could reach hers.

The tingling of our connection sprang to life. It was so much stronger than before the kiss. Ugh, my body responded to the prick. I scowled at him. "My *friends* call me Ronnie." I pointed at her. "And I think we'll be good friends, seeing as she doesn't want to attack me for my blood." Wait. Would she? I looked at Sierra. "Right?"

"Definitely not." She snickered and wrapped an arm around my shoulder. "The biggest threat I am to you is that I might want to do your makeup and dress you. Your hair is gorgeous."

"Maybe I'll take my chances with being bitten." The thought of Alex nibbling on my lip heated my body. "I hate makeup."

Sierra arched an eyebrow. "Don't let the vampire prince get in your mind."

"Vampire *prince*?" I squeaked. That seemed important. Any thoughts of us being together, which had been crazy to begin with, vanished. His level of dishonesty cut me. "Something else you didn't tell me."

"What do you want from me?" Alex placed a hand on

his chest. "I was about to tell you everything before these four dogs showed up."

"That's it," Griffin muttered, but I didn't even glance at him.

My vision hazed as I glared at Alex. "This would've been good to know before you *kissed me*."

"Okay," Sterlyn cut in and motioned toward the city. "We've caught people's attention, so we need to leave. Why don't you two continue this conversation back at our house? That way, we'll be there in case someone tries something with her." She waved her hand at me. "And no one will get upset with you being in Shadow Ridge."

"Fine." Alex inhaled sharply. "Ronnie and I will meet you there."

"It's Veronica to you." I had to draw a line between us, even if it was a thin line. It would keep our relationship in perspective, and I needed all the help I could get.

Killian laughed loudly. "Dude, I almost feel sorry for you, and that says a lot since we're like mortal enemies and all."

Alex hissed.

"Are you comfortable riding with him?" Sterlyn asked. "You're more than welcome to ride with us."

I wanted to ride with Alex, proving how little I valued my life. I should have wanted to stay far away from him, yet, here I was, wanting to stay right beside him. "Um ..."

"I promise you're safe with me," he vowed, staring at me with such intensity that my lips tingled. *Again.* "I would never harm you. You should know that by now."

"From the one day you've known each other?" Sierra deadpanned.

"You know—" he began, red mixing with the soft blue of his eyes.

Apparently, when he got angry, his vampire bled through. I didn't need a fight to break out. "No, I'll ride with him. It'll give him a chance to fill in more blanks."

"Are you sure?" Griffin asked as he scanned my face. "Don't let him pressure you."

"It's fine." There was nowhere else I'd rather be, and I wanted a few more minutes with him. Besides, my chest hurt at the thought of him not being next to me. Once everything got straightened out, I would never see him again. "I promise. I have my phone if I need you."

"Stay right behind us," Sterlyn warned Alex. She gazed at me. "If anything seems off ..."

"Got it." Surprisingly, Alex didn't sound as angry, though.

We headed back to the vehicles, and I climbed into the passenger side of the Mercedes. Silence descended between us as I replayed the conversation in my mind. When he pulled out onto the main road, I realized our alone time was dwindling.

"When you said he's lost most of his humanity, what did you mean?" He couldn't gloss over information any longer. That wasn't how this worked. "Are you saying he's more dangerous than a normal vampire?"

"There are no normal vampires." Alex glanced in the rearview mirror. "Every vampire starts out with humanity. Depending on our choices, we either keep it or change over to the feral side."

"What kind of choices?" I rubbed my lip where he'd bitten me. "Bite or kill someone?"

"It's more than just biting," he answered as his eyes flicked to my lips. "What I did to you didn't put me at risk because I wasn't feeding from you or hurting you. But what Eilam is doing to your friend isn't right. He's toying with her for his pleasure. He's hurting her both physically and emotionally by making her think she enjoys it."

My throat and chest tightened as I held back a scream. Maybe I shouldn't have asked because I didn't know what to do. "How do we save her?"

"Matthew is working on it. That's why I was at the bar last night. We're trying to figure out who, out of our population of over one thousand that we're responsible for, has become more like Eilam. Things are beginning to spiral out of control." Alex focused back on the road. "He'll jail Eilam to find out who is involved and force him to reset your friend's mind."

I hated that she'd been manipulated, but her remembering it all might be worse. "Do you think you can make her forget everything?"

He glanced at me. "You got mad at me for trying to erase your memory, but you want us to do it to her?"

Dammit, he had me there. "You're right, but Annie has her entire future mapped out. She's going to be a lawyer and help foster kids like us. I'd hate for this to change that."

He huffed and pinched the bridge of his nose. "If that's what you want, I'll see what I can do."

"So your brother will put her mind right, and she and I can go home?" Part of me filled with hope and the other part dread. Ever since I'd met him, my insides had been at war.

"Probably not." He sighed. "Only the vampire who has manipulated someone's mind can undo it. I'm guessing Eilam won't be willing to do it right away. He'll have to be kept in jail and starved for a few days before he'll agree to it."

I wasn't sure whether I was relieved or not. I'd have more time here with him—and with Sterlyn. My fear was that the longer I stayed, the harder it would be for me to leave them behind. "How often does the mind manipulation fail on humans?" He'd seemed so surprised that my memory had stayed intact, so it couldn't be too frequent.

"Never." He sighed. "You're the first human I've heard of it not working on."

The answer sat hard on me.

The ride back to Sterlyn's seemed too short. We were already turning into her neighborhood, proving I enjoyed his company way more than I should have. "What will happen to Annie until then?"

"She'll stay at his house." He frowned. "That's the only place she'll want to be, so she can wait for his return."

"Alone?" I didn't like the sound of that. "What about his friends or family?"

"He lives alone, so we got lucky there." He pulled into the driveway and shifted the car into park.

His *we* warmed my heart more than it should have. He sounded invested in my problem, which threatened to open my heart to him more. "If anything happens to her ..." I trailed off, unable to finish my thought.

"Nothing will." He turned to me and gently cupped my face in his hands while his blue eyes stared intently into mine. "I promise you. I will do whatever it takes to keep you both safe. You have my word."

I believed him.

Wholeheartedly.

That couldn't be wise when dealing with a vampire.

He'd lowered his head, his eyes locked on my lips, when something banged on my window.

CHAPTER THIRTEEN

I yelped and jerked around, the magic of the moment dissipating. Sierra was peeking inside, wearing a shit-eating grin across her face as she waggled her brows.

"Whatcha doin'?" She tried to school her expression, but her smirk broke into a large smile as she enjoyed catching Alex and me in a near kiss.

Worse, I hated that she'd interrupted us. I should have been thankful, not annoyed. "Nothing," I said curtly. I grabbed the door handle and pushed it open, nudging her out of the way.

She danced away like she'd expected it.

Damn supernaturals.

"Just ignore her," Killian said as he wrapped an arm around Sierra's shoulders. He tucked her into his chest and gave her a noogie.

"Stop!" she squealed and tried to get out of his arms, but he held her tight. Her hair was messy from the friction.

"You don't give someone you just met a hard time." He grunted with brotherly affection. "It's called *boundaries.* You should learn them sometime."

"Hey, I don't like being boxed in or trapped." She giggled and punched him in the stomach. He loosened his arms, and she took several steps back and lifted her hands in victory.

Sterlyn looked at me and frowned as if she was aware of my feelings.

But that was impossible.

"I'd better go," Alex said.

I wanted to throw a tantrum, but that wouldn't change anything. He needed to go so I could get my head on straight, even if I'd feel empty inside.

"Let's go inside and give them a second to say good-bye." Sterlyn motioned for her companions to follow her.

"You're going to leave her alone out here with him?" Griffin sounded shocked. "We raced to get her from Shadow Terrace."

Alex growled, and I winced.

I should've waited longer before texting her, but I'd been freaked out after learning that vampires existed, let alone that I was attracted to one. Griffin had every right to be annoyed with me.

"True, but he is helping her get her sister back. We can't do it without causing a ton of problems." Sterlyn arched an eyebrow at her boyfriend. "She'll yell if she needs us." She glanced back at me. "Right?"

"Uh, yeah." She was giving me a chance to tell her to stay, but despite my brain screaming at me, I wanted a few more minutes to talk to Alex alone.

"I won't be long." I tried to sound confident. I didn't want to piss them off when they'd already done so much for me.

Griffin scowled at Alex and warned, "One wrong move,

and I don't care if you're a member of the council or vampire royalty."

"Noted." Alex rubbed his fingers together but said nothing else.

Sierra leaned over the car door. "Are you sure you want to stay? Blink twice for yes."

"Uh ... yes." I hadn't expected that request. "Why would I need to blink?"

"In case he messed with your mind." She lifted her hands. "I'm not sure how that all works, but I was thinking maybe you verbally couldn't say no."

"Wait ..." Hope blossomed in my chest. "Could Annie still be aware?"

"No, that's not how it works." Alex scratched the back of his neck. "I'm sorry." He frowned at Sierra.

"In fairness, I didn't know." She pursed her lips. "It was an honest question."

"Come on." Killian grabbed Sierra's arm and tugged her toward the house.

She stumbled after him and mouthed *just yell* as the four of them entered through the garage.

Though I'd only just met her, I already felt a kinship with her akin to the one I felt with Sterlyn. All my life, I'd remained wary of new people, keeping them at arm's length. It had taken me months to warm up to Eliza and Annie, so to feel a connection with not only Sterlyn and Sierra but Alex, too, in such a short span of time made my head spin.

Of course, that would happen with supernaturals. I couldn't click like that with mere mortals.

Figured.

"They are too much at times," Alex grumbled and shook his head. "Especially Sierra. She just couldn't give us another moment."

The door shut, and we were alone again.

"And what will another moment have accomplished?" I tried not to look at him, but I couldn't be a coward. Given the way he was reacting, he had to feel something toward me too. Or that could be wishful thinking.

He sighed and said, "You're right. Prolonging this will make the inevitable that much harder."

Although I was thinking the same thing, his confirmation cut deep, and I reacted with anger. "How many does this make?"

"What do you mean?" he asked, his forehead lining with confusion.

"How many girls have you done this to?" I gestured between us. He was gorgeous and could alter minds. There was no telling how many girls he'd kissed or slept with *in three hundred years* without needing to worry about the awkward conversation afterward. Well, until me.

"Done what to who?" He surveyed the surroundings. "I feel like I'm missing part of this conversation."

"You kissed me and tried to make me forget about it!" If he wanted me to spell it out, I would. "You were at a loss when it didn't work. So ... how often do you do that?"

He stiffened as his attention flicked back to my face. "Is that a legitimate question?"

"I just asked it." He wouldn't make me feel bad about it. "You tried messing with my memories. You owe me an answer."

He scoffed. "It's downright insulting that you think I'd do that lightly. Hell, my brother is pissed at me over you. This is the first time I've ever gone against his wishes. He is my king."

"Oh, so this is my fault?" I let anger course through me,

preferring to feel that over the longing and hurt. "You're the one who kissed me in that bar, not the other way around."

"And if I hadn't claimed you, then one of the other jack-asses would've." His lip curled in disgust. "I was doing you a favor."

Now that I was aware of this world, I needed answers. "What does being claimed mean?"

He deflated. "That's what vampires who've lost their humanity do. As I said, my kind is selfish in nature, so those *people* tag humans as their property, and they're off-limits to any other vampire who might consider feeding off them."

Now people thought I belonged to him. The thought didn't repulse me, warning me of its toxicity. I had to put my foot down. "Too bad you couldn't make me forget." We were goading each other, but I couldn't shut my mouth. He brought out the worst in me. "The kiss was subpar to begin with."

"Don't lie." Alex sneered, looking sexy as hell. "I smelled your arousal, and you climbed all over me in the bar."

He had me there, and I hated it. "I didn't hear you complain."

"How could I when your mouth was fused to mine?" A vein in his neck bulged. "I'm too gentlemanly to embarrass you in front of the others."

"And outside your car before you tried to erase my memory?" If he was going to blame me, then I'd make him admit he felt something for me too. "What's your excuse for that kiss? Because no one was around."

"A momentary lapse in judgment." His breathing quick-ened, and pink infused with the blue in his irises, proving he was as angry as me. "You're human, and I'm a prince. Being tied to someone like you would weaken my family's position and encourage others to take a human as their pet. Things couldn't work out between us anyway."

And there was the truth—something neither of us could contradict, no matter how much I wanted to. "You're right." Staying in the car, arguing with him, was like talking to a wall.

Pointless.

Hopeless.

And only caused me more pain.

The best thing to do was get out and march into the house, but I had to make sure he would still help me with Annie. I inhaled deeply to calm my ass down. "I'm not trying to be a jerk."

"You aren't?" His eyebrows arched so high they about disappeared into his hairline. "Because this entire conversation happened because of you."

Ugh, he had to keep digging. I was pretty sure he wanted to fight with me as much as I wanted to argue with him. We were trying to stay enraged instead of addressing whatever wafted between us. Bitterness filled my mouth, but I swallowed it down and tried to keep a clear head. "It's just ... Annie." In fairness, the magnitude of my feelings was partially due to her situation.

"Got it," he said coldly and gestured to the door. "Yes, all that matters is your *sister*. I better get going to make sure nothing else happens to her."

Gathering what remained of my wits, I left the car. Before I shut the door, I leaned over. "Please make sure she stays safe."

"Don't worry." He put the car in reverse. "I'll do it even if it kills me since, clearly, that wouldn't bother you."

I slammed the door shut, channeling all my rage into the resounding *crack*.

The Mercedes squealed out of the driveway and lurched forward, speeding toward the neighborhood entrance. Even though I'd provoked him on purpose, I couldn't budge. My legs were frozen as I watched him leave. A little bit of regret replaced my fury.

Fine. Okay. I was in denial ...

A lot of regret replaced my fury.

"Are you okay?" Sterlyn asked, startling me.

I spun around to find her standing on the front porch, leaning against one of the white columns with her lips pressed into a line.

"You just went inside."

"I heard the door slam and came to check on you." She walked to me soundlessly. "Things seemed tense between you two."

She wasn't kidding. "Is it that obvious?"

"I knew something was different last night when he brought you to our house." She tilted her head, examining me. "I thought it was a ploy to get a read on us, but after talking to you and seeing your distress, I realized he'd brought you here out of concern for your safety."

"And that's weird?" The question fell out, and I regretted asking. No matter her answer, it wouldn't be good.

"Very." She shifted her weight to one leg. "Vampires, in general, are selfish. They don't do things for others unless it's to benefit their own agenda."

"Like favors?"

She nodded. "But what he doesn't know is that I would've let you stay without him giving up a favor. You're a good person, and I think we were destined to become friends."

I agreed with her, which was problematic for me. "I can find somewhere else to stay tonight. Apparently, it might take a couple of days before the vampire agrees to restore Annie's mind." A chill ran through me. I sincerely hoped Alex would follow through on my request. I didn't want Annie to remember the hell she had to be going through with Eilam.

"Nonsense." Sterlyn shook her head. "You will stay here with us. If any of the other vampires figure out how Alex feels about you, you'll be in more danger than before."

"I'm pretty sure he hates me." And rightfully so. I'd been a jerk to him, but that was best for both of us. The more time we spent together, the harder it would be when whatever this was between us ended.

I had to ensure I remained standing.

Sterlyn chuckled. "Not by a long shot. You two are connected. There's no other explanation. He just needs time to figure things out, especially with his brother. Even though I haven't been here long, I've noticed that Alex does everything for Matthew, so admitting you two are connected goes against his very nature."

I bit my tongue to keep more questions from tumbling out. I had a feeling the truth would make this situation even crazier and more complicated. For the first time, I decided that living in ignorance was best.

"Come on." Sterlyn looped her arm through mine. "Rosemary is on her way, and Sierra is picking out a movie. Let's get settled inside before the inevitable argument over what we're going to watch gets too heated."

At a loss as to what else to do, I followed her inside.

I spent the next week in a daze, but it was time to do the inevitable. With dread, I picked up my cell phone and pressed Eliza's number. I'd never dreaded calling her before, but I was experiencing many firsts here lately.

I paced the bedroom as the phone rang.

She picked up immediately. "Ronnie, I've been so worried. Is everything okay? There's been so much turmoil with you."

"What do you mean?" The last sentence sounded odd, as if she sensed what was going on down here.

She laughed awkwardly, which also wasn't normal. "Well, there must be since you haven't called in days."

I guessed that made sense. "Yeah, sorry. It's been hectic. Annie doesn't want to leave her ... er ... boyfriend, and I told her I wasn't leaving unless she came with me. Things are tense." I tried to explain without lying. She deserved better than that. "I had to quit my job, though, seeing as I couldn't commit to a return date."

"Maybe I should come down there," she said hesitantly.

"No!" I said too eagerly. Exposing her to all this at her age would be horrendous. I was having a hard enough time wrapping my head around it. I could only imagine how she would feel. I had to protect her like she'd protected me for the past five years. "I think Annie would feel ganged up on, and it might make things worse."

"You're right." Eliza sighed. "How'd your boss take it? I know he considered you one of the best servers."

That he did, which was a blessing for me. "He wasn't thrilled, but he knows this is unlike me and that something important is going on. He emphasized that when things calm down, I'll still have a place at Sergino's."

"Good." Eliza sounded relieved. "I'll be glad when you two get back home. I miss you. Annie, too."

"I miss you too, and I feel the same." I winced, realizing that the thought of leaving here didn't sit well with me. The longer I stayed with Sterlyn and the others, the more I didn't want to leave, even though I didn't sleep well, my mind weighed down with thoughts of Annie and Alex.

"All right." Shuffling noise came from her end. "I've got to get to work but call me if you need anything or have an update."

"O—" But I stopped, the line already dead. I rolled my eyes at Eliza's habit of simply hanging up when she was done talking. At least, some things never changed.

I had no idea when I'd have a real update for her. The last I'd heard, Annie was still brainwashed.

Alex had told me it would be several days before she was back to normal, but I was getting antsy. Sterlyn had taken the week off at the coffee shop to keep me company, and I was forever thankful. I couldn't imagine the state I'd have been in if I'd been alone every day.

Yet another mind-blowing event had been meeting Rosemary, who was an angel, of all things. I'd felt an instant connection with her, and she'd obviously felt the same toward me, because Sierra had muttered that it had taken weeks before the angel had said more than a few words to her, so how were Rosemary and I getting along so well already?

I sighed and put my phone in my pocket then headed into the living room to join the group.

"I swear, I'm growing tired of these silly films." Rosemary leaned forward to see Sierra's face. Her long mahogany hair fell past her shoulders as her purplish twilight eyes narrowed.

I took a seat in the middle of the long couch between Rosemary and Killian with Sierra on the floor. She shuffled over to use my legs as a backrest. Sterlyn and Griffin always claimed the loveseat where they cuddled for the entire evening.

"We have enough fighting and scorn in our life," Sierra retorted as she glanced over her shoulder at the angel. "We deserve laughter."

Every night since I'd been here, we'd watched a romantic comedy that always left me feeling raw. Each kissing scene or romantic gesture put Alex at the forefront of my mind.

The jackass.

"From here on out, I'm voting with the guys." Rosemary gestured to Killian and Griffin. "I'm so tired of watching the same plot over and over, just with another whimpering girl."

"That's fine." Sierra stood and placed her hands on her hips. "Now that we have Ronnie, that'll make it a draw, which automatically goes in the girls' favor."

"How is that even fair?" Killian groaned. "This whole system is rigged."

"How do you know she'd vote with you?" Rosemary faced me. "She could surprise you."

"My girl has me." Sierra patted her chest and gestured to me. "Don't you?"

Shit. Caught in the middle where I hated to be. But the thought of watching another one of those movies sounded too damn painful. "Rosemary has a point ..."

"What?" Sierra's eyes widened, and her mouth dropped open. "You've got to be kidding me! You're supposed to be my girl."

"I am." And I meant it, which took me by surprise. "But maybe something less kissy and grittier?"

"We've found the missing part of our group." Griffin closed his eyes and smiled. "I knew we kept her around for a reason."

"Sterlyn!" Sierra whined.

"You've had a good run." She grimaced and shrugged.

Killian stood, his face full of tension.

"Don't be so dramatic, Kill." Sierra rolled her eyes. "Fine, we'll watch one of those actiony movies tomorrow, okay?"

"No, it's not that." His expression remained tense as he glanced at Griffin, then Sterlyn. "A vampire just crossed our threshold in the woods behind our house."

CHAPTER FOURTEEN

"I thought vampires were allowed in Shadow Ridge." Killian's tension put me on edge. I still didn't fully understand the rules of who could be where, and I'd avoided asking too many questions about vampires because that invoked more thoughts of Alex. But I wanted to know everything to an unhealthy level. I'd bitten my tongue way too many times to prevent myself from asking about them.

"All the supernaturals are allowed in town because of the university, but no one, not even another wolf shifter, is allowed to visit the woods behind another pack's property without permission," Rosemary said as she stood, towering over me. All of them were taller than me, with Sterlyn being the tallest girl but still shorter than the guys, Griffin having an inch or two on Killian. "Trespassing is rude, not to mention threatening around here. Everyone knows that."

Sierra exhaled. "What have we told you about manners?"

"No, it's fine." She'd stated the obvious, and I felt dumb, but she had a point. "I like her that way."

"Oh, dear God." Sierra slumped. "Don't encourage her."

"Should we contact Alex?" Of course, at the first opportunity, I'd bring him up. "He's the prince, after all. That has to mean something."

"He'll only get involved if he can gain something." Rosemary sneered. "His parents were the same way and raised their kids to follow in their footsteps. Even Gwen has to make a point of telling Matthew everything she sees—especially in her classes—to gain more favor with him."

Griffin untangled from Sterlyn and climbed to his feet. "Why don't you guys stay here while Killian and I check things out?"

Sierra stuck her tongue out. "Aw, the big burly man is trying to take care of the wee womenfolk."

"What if it's a trap?" Sterlyn ignored her and shook her head. "I don't think that's smart. They might want us to split up and leave Ronnie exposed."

"I agree with Sterlyn." Rosemary crossed her arms. "We should stay together."

"We can't just stay here and hope they pass through." Killian scowled. "They need to know we saw them sneaking around on our land even if they don't plan to attack."

Then it clicked. This group was used to facing danger together. My presence had complicated things.

"You're overthinking it." Rosemary dropped her arms. "Ronnie can go with us. I'll keep an eye on her. If things go south, I'll take her somewhere safe. But leaving her alone in the house isn't an option, and neither is a handful of us running out there."

"Whoa." Sierra held out her arms. "Are the guards on their way? Isn't this what they're supposed to take care of?"

"First off, I'm the head of the guards, so I should go out

there," Killian said. "Besides, there's only one on duty now that things have calmed down. I'll order him to watch the tree line in case more vampires come." Killian marched to the back door. "It'll take a few minutes for the guards to get here, and it could be too late if we don't get a move on."

"Fine, we'll go with Rosemary's plan." Sterlyn walked past Griffin to the back door. "We'll all go, but Ronnie needs to stay in the center. If there are more than a few vampires, Rosemary will take her and Sierra to the bar, and they can hang out until the fight is over."

"Great." Sierra wrapped an arm around my waist. "Lump me in with the human."

"Your fighting is subpar." Rosemary rubbed her nose. "Most of the time, you're a liability."

Sierra glared at me. "See, that's on you. You've encouraged her to be her blunt self."

Even in this dire moment, a smile threatened to cross my face. Which *couldn't* be normal. "Better than her sugar-coating it."

"I like sugar." Sierra motioned to herself. "Lots of it. Don't ruin it for the rest of us."

Opening the door, Killian locked eyes with me. "The more you engage with the crazy, the longer she'll keep going."

That wasn't hard to believe. "Got it. Ignore Sierra."

"Hey," she gasped and bared her teeth.

Sterlyn and Griffin rushed out the door first with Sierra and me behind them. Killian and Rosemary took up the rear.

The half-moon had risen above the tree line where its glow cascaded over us. This place was beautiful, and maybe when things calmed down, I could find the time to go for a hike and enjoy the natural beauty of the area. I loved exploring nature but didn't have a chance to do it back home.

A shimmer caught my eye, and I nearly stopped to stare. I'd never noticed that Sterlyn's hair seemed brighter under the moonlight or that her skin glowed silver. Her eyes looked more silver than purple as if the moon magnified something inside her. She reminded me of an angel, and when I glanced at Rosemary, her skin also emanated a faint glow.

We moved at a steady pace through the backyard toward the oaks and maple trees. Squirrels scurried away, and owls hooted in the distance. The comforting woodsy scent washed over me. If Killian hadn't told me that a vampire was lurking nearby, I wouldn't have sensed anything out of the ordinary.

All five of my companions were tense, emphasizing that danger was near.

Sierra sniffed and scanned our surroundings.

I wasn't sure if she was searching for a scent or had picked up on one, but I kept my mouth shut. I didn't need to alert whoever was out here to our presence—if they didn't already know.

I wasn't sure what supernatural abilities they had, but Alex had heard the Navigator before me, so they likely had enhanced hearing.

Thick trees surrounded us, and Sterlyn pointed to our left before pivoting and taking off in that direction.

We all had to move faster to keep up with her. I'd never run so fast before, and the trees blurred past until a dull ache caught me in the side.

Great, that was how out of shape I was.

I tried pushing through, but the pain turned sharp and

stabby. Unable to maintain the pace, I slowed, forcing Rosemary and Killian to slow as well.

"Dammit, move," Rosemary demanded.

"I need to catch my breath." I leaned over, taking deep gulps of air. Darkness crept into the edges of my vision, making me feel more fatigued.

No matter how much air I inhaled, I couldn't catch my breath. Then a *yank*ing took hold. It took every ounce of concentration I had not to run straight into danger.

"Are you okay?" Sierra asked with concern. "Are you going to have a heart attack?"

"Out ... of ... shape." I doubted she could relate. For all I knew, supernaturals didn't get out of breath. "I don't exercise much."

The back of my neck tingled, forcing me to straighten. The *yank* took a stronger hold over me. Sterlyn and Griffin had stopped about thirty feet away. Sterlyn glanced back at us.

They must have regretted bringing me. Not only was I slowing them down, but I'd made us easy targets. "I'm—"

"Shh," Sierra whispered. All traces of her usual mirth had vanished as her attention focused on a section of the trees between Sterlyn, Griffin, and us.

Rosemary stepped between Sierra and me and grabbed our arms as huge black wings exploded from her back. I blinked in amazement. The moon reflected off her feathers, giving them an iridescent look that contrasted with her glowing fair skin. I wanted to touch a feather but figured that would be crossing a personal line.

Someone stepped out from between the trees. Sterlyn sped forward, grabbed them by the neck, then slammed them against the tree.

Alex's startled face came into view.

The urge to run to him exploded inside me, but my legs didn't move.

As Rosemary flapped her wings, the realization that I wouldn't get to hear him out compelled me into action. As she lifted both Sierra and me into the air, I tried to twist out of her grasp, but she had an iron hold on my arm, and my feet lifted off the ground until we hovered ten feet in the air.

"Sterlyn, stop," Alex gasped before she cut off his airway.

"Stop?" she demanded. "You were sneaking up on us. Did you think we'd allow you to break our laws? How would you like it if we went nosing around your side of the river?"

"I wasn't up to anything or planning to attack," he rasped. "You'd know if I was lying."

Her hold loosened. "Then why are you sneaking through the woods in our backyard?"

His attention landed on me. "Because I wanted to check on her."

"That doesn't make any sense," Rosemary said but paused her ascent. "Vampires don't care about anyone."

Unease prickled through me. Alex had promised to help me with Annie, and he was here instead. Had he come to give me bad news, or was he bored with babysitting her? Either scenario wasn't good.

"Yeah, they don't." Griffin chewed on his fingernail. "But he's been protecting Ronnie since she got here."

"I'm not here to cause trouble." Alex raised his hands. "I'm not even fighting you."

"Fine." Sterlyn released her hold but didn't step aside. "Just know that Ronnie is under our protection, so any injury to her will cause problems between the wolves and the vampires."

"Are you sure we can trust him?" Rosemary's wings flapped slowly, keeping us suspended. "Maybe others are coming and he's trying to distract."

"It's just me." Alex ran his hands through his hair. "I didn't think about how this would look. I didn't think it through."

"Think what through?" Killian asked as he walked underneath Rosemary, Sierra, and me, moving closer to Alex. "Sneaking into our neighborhood? Not saying anything when you got close? Or not coming to the front door and knocking like any sane person would do?"

"Yes." Sierra flailed. "All that."

"And you said you didn't like blunt." I arched an eyebrow and stared at my mouthy new friend. "And preferred sugar-coating."

"Only when it comes to anything aimed at me."

Rosemary lowered us to the ground and muttered, "And I thought she and Killian were bad together. The two of them act like sisters."

"And how would you know that?" Sierra challenged. "You're an only child."

"Mom told me enough stories about her and my uncle." Rosemary released her grip and grimaced. "Sorry, Sterlyn."

"It's fine." Sterlyn smiled sadly. "You don't need to feel bad about mentioning him."

If my desire to know why Alex was here hadn't been so strong, I'd have asked about what Rosemary had said. But Alex was here for a reason. "Is Annie okay?"

"Yes, she's still at Eilam's house." Alex might have been trying to reassure me, but it fell flat.

"Then why are you here?" Was she alone? What if Eilam's friends did something to her? "I can't believe you left her unprotected."

"Matthew is there. No one would dare defy him to his face." Alex rubbed his neck. "We vampires are more the backstabbing type, so she's safe."

"Your brother, who was ready to attack me at Thirsty's bar?" That did not make me feel any better. I was pretty sure Annie had a better chance with the vampire who'd messed with her mind.

"Things are getting way out of hand over there." Griffin clenched his hands. "You can't attack humans."

"He didn't." Alex pulled at his hair. "He was mad at me because I'd claimed her in front of everyone."

"First off, you aren't supposed to be *claiming humans*. It's against the law, and now the *prince* has done it? That sets a horrible precedent." Rosemary wagged a finger. "Second, he's old enough to have more self-restraint. Maybe we should bring this up with the council."

This entire situation was insane, and I was the main cause. Well, other than Alex sneaking around in the woods to watch me.

Yeah, when I said it that way, it was definitely creepy.

"You don't think I know that!" Alex exclaimed. "Matthew has forced me to parade around town so everyone can see that my humanity is still intact, and that Veronica hasn't been around me. He's threatening to detain me in Shadow City if I don't fall in line. But I'm telling you, if I hadn't claimed her that day, someone else would have!"

"Still not smart, dude." Griffin exhaled. "You're a leader."

"I'm well aware," Alex hissed. "And I reacted to *protect* her."

"How is the situation going, beyond the hiccup?" Sterlyn asked, reining in the conversation.

"Like I said, we're taking care of the situation." Alex

massaged his temples. "My actions did put a bump in our plans. Matthew almost lost it because he thought I'd decided to join Eilam's followers. But I didn't feed off her."

Join Eilam's followers? I had so many damn questions. Alex had nipped my lip, but I'd seen Eilam drink from Annie. Alex definitely hadn't done *that*.

"I'm still stuck on why you're sneaking around back here," Killian said, pushing the issue. "Because that's seriously not cool, man. You know why we're extra cautious."

"You're right. I'm sorry." Alex stepped around Sterlyn, so he was in the center of the group. "Veronica and I didn't leave on the best of terms, and I hadn't heard from any of you. I wanted to make sure everything was all right."

"And you couldn't pick up the phone?" Sierra rubbed her hands together.

Alex's face turned pink. "That would've been the smart thing to do, but Annie fell asleep, and I wanted to get away, given how hard Matthew has been riding my ass. I thought I'd do a quick run by before Matthew noticed I'd gone."

My heart thawed, and my body inched toward him of its accord. Anger was easier to handle. Without it, I stopped remembering why it was such a horrible idea to be around him. "So she's okay?"

His soft blue eyes warmed as he looked at me. "Relatively speaking, she's fine. She talks about you in her dreams, but when she's awake, she's frantic for Eilam."

"But she remembers me." She had to if she was dreaming about me. "That's good, right?"

"Yes, although it's not normal." Alex's face softened. "Usually, when someone's mind is that messed with, even their dreams don't allow them to escape. Your sister must be very strong because I've never seen that prior to you."

Hell yeah, she was strong. That prick had probably

been trying to brainwash her since the day she saw him. "I don't know if I should be relieved or more upset."

"Relieved." He licked his lips as he came closer to me, and his sweet maple scent scattered my wits. "Even though it's been a huge issue for me."

I shouldn't ask, but I couldn't not ask either. "How so?"

My words hung between us, and it was like only Alex and I were there.

"Because it's hard enough not to think about you." He brushed my cheek. "To hear her talk about you makes you more real."

Butterflies took flight in my belly, and I tamped them down. It did no good.

"Uh ... this is very awkward." Killian cleared his throat. "I feel weird watching them, but I'd feel weirder turning my back."

"Right," Sierra jumped in. "And if they're that bad when we're watching, I don't wanna know what they would do with our backs turned."

Those two knew how to ruin a moment, which was both a blessing and a curse.

Alex closed his eyes and exhaled. "I should get back. I'll return with an update when there's one to give. As of now, Eilam is holding out, despite his hunger."

"Come to the front door next time," Griffin warned. "Or Sterlyn might rip out your throat."

"Noted." Alex nodded and stared at me a moment longer. "Sorry to cause trouble."

"Be safe." Sterlyn patted his arm, and he turned and headed deeper into the woods.

I had to lock down my legs and will myself not to follow him.

Once he was out of sight, we silently walked back to the

house. Rosemary and Sterlyn kept exchanging glances, but I didn't have the energy to ask about the internal conversation I was sure they were having. They'd seen the weird chemistry between Alex and me, and I didn't know why it existed or want to explain it.

Exhaustion tugged at me. All I wanted to do was crawl into bed.

"Why don't you go inside and get some rest." Sterlyn smiled sweetly. "We'll stay out here and keep watch a little longer and talk to the guards who are arriving."

Yeah, they wanted to talk about me, but whatever. For once, I didn't care to hear what they had to say. "Good night."

Sierra frowned, clearly not happy, but Sterlyn grinned and said, "Good night."

I waved at them and entered the house, heading for my room before they could start probing.

Not bothering to turn on the lights, I plopped backward onto the bed and stared at the ceiling. After seeing Alex tonight, I wouldn't be getting him off my mind.

A sweet smell hit my nose, and my heart raced. The idiot hadn't left. Instead, he'd snuck into my room. I should have been pissed, but I was too excited.

"Alex?" I whispered, not wanting the others to hear.

"Not quite." A dark chuckle came from right beside me. "But close."

CHAPTER FIFTEEN

"**K**lyn?" I squeaked. I would never forget that voice. I'd opened my mouth to scream when the bed dipped beside me and he sat, his stark red eyes focused on mine. His hand covered my mouth as his irises glowed against the darkness, terrifying me. "One noise and I'll make sure something else happens to Annie."

My limbs had frozen to the bed with fear, and I wasn't sure I was breathing. My mind couldn't wrap around how this asshole had gotten into my room.

"Ahh ..." he purred. "You remember me. I'm so glad." He tilted his head. "We don't have long, but I'm feeling generous. As long as you promise not to scream, I'll let you talk. But one noise I don't like, and I'll text my friends and put a plan into action for dear, sweet Annie." He smiled sinisterly. "Do we have a deal?"

I nodded, wanting his nasty hands off me. He had to know I wouldn't do anything that would put Annie at risk. "How did you get in here?"

"I saw the prince leave town and followed him." He rubbed his fingertips along my arm, and goosebumps rose, not from pleasure but from fear and loathing. "He was so distracted that he didn't notice me. When he pulled off the road right before the entrance to this neighborhood, I thought it might be where he had stashed you."

He paused as if waiting for my reaction.

My eyes had adjusted to the near darkness of the room, and I could make out his features.

He sniffed. "Mmm ... your fear makes you smell even more delicious."

If I didn't keep my emotions in check, he would attack me sooner, and I wouldn't be able to call for help. The longer I held him off, the sooner Sterlyn and the others would come back into the house and figure out something was wrong.

As he sniffed, he leaned over me. "The wolves were so focused on Alex that I was able to sneak inside while you all were out."

With control I didn't realize I had, I steadied my breathing and forced myself not to think about what would inevitably happen. "You won't get out of here without getting caught." My voice shook, but it sounded somewhat strong.

"Maybe, but after Alex claimed you when you should have been mine ..." He closed his eyes as his fingernails dug into my skin. "For that, I have no choice but to make you mine, no matter the consequences."

Warm blood trickled down my arm, and Klyn inhaled deeply.

He lowered his head to my arm as his cool tongue darted out, licking my blood before it could drip onto the sheets. "As long as you don't scream, we'll take this slow, and I'll make it feel good. But if you call for help, I'll make it fast and painful then take out all my frustration on Annie.

It's totally up to you, but either way, you will be mine. The royal family has taken enough from us."

"Yours? What do you mean?" I needed to keep him talking because there was no way in hell I'd let that happen. But I had to be careful about how I got out of this situation.

Something flickered in my peripheral vision, and I looked toward it. A chill ran down my spine. The shadow had appeared at the window and was watching the scene unfold. And unless fear had affected my senses more than I knew, I wasn't imagining it.

He chuckled. "You were mine that night. I was in the process of claiming you until that superior jackass of a prince intervened." He ran a finger down my cheek, and I shivered with disgust. "Vampires are meant to drink from humans, and the royal family has tried to keep our urges in check for too long. We will rise above and take the royal family down when enough of us are strong enough and embrace what we really are. "Don't worry." He lapped the blood from my arm again then straddled me, pinning me down to the bed. "I'll influence your mind so you can enjoy it too. And I'll make sure I drink every ounce of your blood as your punishment." His eyes glowed like Alex's when he'd tried to mess with my mind.

In a way, I was glad Alex had tried to influence me already, despite it pissing me off. At least, I didn't have to worry about becoming his puppet, and that put me in a great spot to surprise Klyn enough so that Sterlyn and the others could come help me. I had to wait for the perfect time.

He leaned toward me and stared deeply into my eyes as he said, "You will enjoy—"

I head-butted him, causing him to fall back, then kicked

him in the crotch. He'd been way too cocky and hadn't considered protecting his sack.

He stiffened, and then his body sagged onto me. His weight kept me from drawing a deep breath to yell.

But hell, they were supernaturals. They should be able to hear me.

I pushed him off me and sucked in enough oxygen to say, "Help!"

"You ..." —Klyn groaned, cupping his balls—"... bitch."

As I scrambled to slip off the bed, he grabbed my arms, tossed me back onto the mattress, and slowly got on top of me.

Dammit, the crotch shot hadn't debilitated him as I'd hoped.

"I'm being attacked!" I yelled as his fangs descended.

The shadow inched closer. My heart pounded so loudly I couldn't hear anything beyond my pulse and Klyn's heavy breathing. I could only hope and pray that the others had heard me. Surely, they had.

He opened his mouth, his fangs elongating, and aimed at my neck.

I punched him. His head jerked, and he missed his mark by a few inches. Frantic, I shoved at his chest to keep him away.

The door crashed open, and light spilled into the room, but I had no clue who had entered. If I took my attention off Klyn, he'd chomp down on me.

He hissed and aimed for my neck again, and between his weight and momentum, I couldn't hold him off.

I waited for the pain from his incisors. Instead, his heavy weight lifted off me.

"You fucking prick," Griffin growled and slammed the vampire into the wall.

My body felt heavy, but the last thing I wanted was to be in this bed. I scrambled to my feet.

All five shifters were in here. They'd all come to protect me. The last bit of the wall I'd put up between me and them crumbled to dust. Whether I liked it or not, these people were my friends. They'd officially earned that title.

The shadow inched away now that the others were with me, and my chest felt even lighter.

Rosemary sneered. "I told you Alex was up to no good."

"He had nothing to do with it," I wheezed. I couldn't stand here and let them think he'd betrayed us. "This asshole followed him and snuck inside while we were distracted."

"We didn't smell him." Sterlyn sniffed and walked across the room to the window, impervious to her boyfriend beating the crap out of the vampire against the wall. She tugged on the window, and the glass rose. It was unlocked. "Well, that's how he got in." She shut and locked it.

We all turned to look at Griffin, who held an unconscious Klyn up by the neck.

"Can we just kill him?" Sierra asked. A coldness wafted off her like I'd never seen before. "Because the prick deserves to die."

I couldn't agree more. He'd been determined to claim me against my will. In fact, he'd been thrilled because I didn't want it.

"If we kill him, that'll cause problems with the council." Sterlyn marched over and stood next to me.

Her proximity eased my concern. "Is the council mostly vampires?"

"No, it's made up of four races, three representatives for each—shifters, vampires, angels, and witches." Sterlyn lifted her hand as if to touch me but dropped it. "As of now, the council's main stance is for each race to take care of its own people and for others not to get involved."

That might have made sense before what had happened here.

"The council has a problem with anything you and Griffin do anyway." Killian cracked his knuckles. "So, it's better to ask for forgiveness than permission."

"Normally, you'd be right." Sterlyn sighed. "But we're already on such thin ice that we can't chance it with the witches or with Azbogah."

"Azbogah?" That was an odd name. "What kind of supernatural is he?"

"An angel," Rosemary growled, "with way too much influence over our community."

"We can't let him go." Killian shook his head. "You know vampires get obsessive. He'll attack her again. What if we aren't close next time?"

I hadn't considered that, but Alex's comment about there being a target on my back now made sense.

"Let's take this one step at a time." Griffin tightened his grip on the vampire's neck. "First, let's call Alex since he seems to feel a connection with her." He nodded at me. "Then we can come up with a schedule so she's never alone."

"That's one reason I called out of work this week." Sterlyn sat on the bed. "I was afraid something like this would happen, yet it still did, even with all of us here."

"Now we know we have to be all humanlike and make sure every damn window and door is shut and locked." Sierra leaned against the wall, glaring at the vampire. "All because of bloodsuckers."

Klyn's face turned a light shade of blue, revealing that the lack of oxygen was affecting him.

I hoped Klyn would die, but they'd agreed not to kill him, so I doubted Griffin would let it go that far. I just hoped he felt *very* uncomfortable.

Sterlyn pulled out her phone, swiped the screen, then placed it to her ear. The room descended into silence.

"Hey, are you still close by?" she asked. After a few seconds of silence, she continued. "We have a problem and need you back here." After another pause, she said, "Yes, she's fine. But a vampire attacked her." She glanced at her phone and placed it back to her ear. "Alex? Are you there?"

"Let me guess; he's not coming." Rosemary leaned back on her heels. "Figures."

"No, he's on his way back." Sterlyn threw the phone onto the bed. "He said he's only five minutes away."

Muscles I hadn't realized I was tensing relaxed, and I feared I knew why. My legs were shaking from the effort to remain standing, but I wasn't ready to go anywhere near the bed. Even though Klyn's attack hadn't been sexual, it had been intimate, and I needed a few more minutes before I could climb back into it. "I'm going to go get a drink of water."

"I'll go with you." Rosemary pointed at the vampire. "Just in case there's another one hiding somewhere."

"Yeah, good point." Killian walked into the hallway. "I'll check the other rooms and make sure everything is locked. We don't need another surprise."

"I'm so sorry, guys." I'd turned their world upside down. I bet they couldn't wait to get rid of me. "I didn't mean to be such a problem."

"You aren't a problem," Sierra said and hugged me. "You keep things interesting. It had gotten boring around here anyway."

"Boring is usually a good thing." I'd never known what

it felt like to be bored until I'd started living at Eliza's. I'd never had the luxury of doing nothing. In all the other places I'd lived, either the foster parents had picked arguments with kids, or other foster kids had grouped together, bullying someone smaller or different.

Being bored meant you were safe.

"Don't get her started." Sterlyn shook her head. "Because she does not believe that."

"Good to know." Not liking being the center of attention, I headed toward the kitchen with Rosemary right behind.

I opened the refrigerator to grab a bottle of water.

Rosemary asked, "Are you okay?"

"I don't know." There was no point in lying. I'd learned they could tell when I did. "I was so stupid. I walked in there without even turning on the light."

"You didn't think you had to." Rosemary shrugged. "No one checks a room when they feel safe. We didn't think to check, and we should've sensed something was off."

"How? He came in through the window."

She and I were so similar. We were both hard on ourselves. I understood why I was that way. For most of my life, I could only count on myself. I wondered what had shaped her.

Rosemary pursed her lips. "Still, we should've been more aware of protecting you."

A loud pounding on the front door interrupted our conversation, and the familiar *yank* occurred in my chest.

"Wow." Rosemary tilted her head from side to side. "I didn't expect Alex to show." She headed through the house to the front door with me trailing behind and swung the door open. She stepped aside without a word to let Alex in.

He pushed through the door, and his gaze found me. He

rushed to me, took the bottle of water out of my hands, and pulled me to him. He rasped, "Are you okay?"

In his arms, I'd never felt safer, and I didn't have the strength to pull away. I was done resisting. The last attack had me wondering why I'd been so resistant in the first place. I buried my head into his chest. Hot tears threatened to spill, but I couldn't let them. I needed to stay as strong as possible until Klyn was gone. He'd get too much of a thrill from seeing me upset.

"Are you hurt?" Alex's tone hardened. "I need to know."

I shook my head. "I was able to fight Klyn off."

"That bastard," he growled as he stepped back and scanned me for wounds.

"If Griffin hadn't gotten there when he did, that vampire would have hurt her, if not worse." Rosemary shut the door. "I was all for killing him, but Sterlyn and Griffin didn't want to cause any more problems with the council."

"How did he get to her?" Alex dropped his hands to his sides. "I left her here, so she'd be safe."

"Says the asshole who tried to sneak through the backyard." Killian strolled into the living room, checking every window.

Alex hissed.

"That is how he got in here." Rosemary seemed all too happy to point the finger at Alex. "While we were distracted by you, he slipped in through her unlocked bedroom window. His smell was contained to her room."

"Where is he?" Alex asked and handed the bottle of water back to me.

"Thanks." Not wanting the three of them to argue further, I waved for him to follow me. "He's still in the bedroom with Griffin and Sterlyn." My survival instincts screamed at me not to go back in, but I couldn't come off as afraid. Everyone here already felt obligated to protect me, and if I broke down like a scared child, I'd only burden them more.

And when someone was a burden, people didn't stick around.

A cool hand caught mine and turned me around. Alex cupped my cheek and kissed my forehead, his closeness calming me.

"You can stay with Rosemary," Alex whispered. "You don't need to go back in there."

"No, I have to." I didn't want to be away from Alex. My head was screaming that he was a vampire and to stay away, but my heart felt safest around him. I was sure even my head knew he'd protect me with his life.

"Please," he pressed. "Let me handle this."

I'd nodded before I even realized I'd agreed.

He kissed my lips sweetly. "I won't be more than a few minutes." Then he headed into the bedroom with Killian following behind.

Rosemary huffed. "And I thought I'd seen everything."

I found her standing only a few feet away. She must have watched the entire exchange.

"I ..." Words couldn't form because I wasn't sure what I was trying to explain.

Her eyes widened, and she strode over and clutched my arm then dragged me back toward the living room.

An alarm rang in my head. "What's wrong? Did Klyn break free?"

My answer came in the form of agonized screams from the bedroom.

CHAPTER SIXTEEN

I tried removing my arm from Rosemary's grasp, but she tightened her hold until my arm tingled from lack of blood flow.

"Please, I have to check on Alex." If I had to beg, I would.

She shook her head. "You can't go in there."

Another pained yelp came from the room and ended in a low guttural cry that abruptly cut off. I didn't need supernatural abilities to hear the gurgling of blood.

Desperation clawed at me, and fresh moisture filled my eyes. "But I have to." I was worried about Alex and the others—I wanted them all safe—but I was also worried about how they would treat Alex. Sterlyn and her friends were a tight group that would risk their lives for one another, but even though they were good people, Alex wasn't in their circle.

"That wasn't Alex." Rosemary clutched my other arm, forcing me to face her. "He's fine."

"And the others too?" I already knew the answer, but I needed to hear it from her.

She nodded. "That was Klyn. Couldn't you tell by the voice?"

Some of my anxiety dissipated. "Human, remember?"

"Unfortunately, I can't forget, or your arm would be broken right now." She lowered her head, and her rosy scent wafted around us. "But you need to calm down, or I'll be forced to restrain you."

Her threat hung over me. I wasn't sure how she'd do it, but I had no doubt she was capable of it. "Klyn tried to get away?" That was stupid, given he was outnumbered. Granted, what kind of guy willingly snuck into a house full of supernaturals? Self-preservation wasn't his strong suit.

Rosemary exhaled, and her fingers dug into my skin as she moved me into the living room. "Not exactly—" She stopped and glanced down the hallway.

I followed her gaze as Sierra appeared.

Her normally light olive complexion was pale. "Uh ... I'm going to stay out here with Ronnie."

"Fine with me. But keep her out here." Rosemary hurried to the bedroom. Her eagerness to get involved with whatever was happening told me she wasn't used to sitting on the sidelines.

Standing in the small foyer, between the front door and the living room, I wrapped my arms around myself. Something had gone south, and I hated being in the dark. "What happened?"

"Let's just say that Klyn is no longer a threat to you." Sierra's face twisted like she tasted something sour. She strolled to the couch and plopped down.

At least, she wasn't as attentive as Rosemary. If I played my cards right, I could sneak away and get back in there. "How so?"

She rubbed her eyes and grimaced. "I haven't seen anything like that."

Yeah, I had to see it for myself, and right now, she was distracted. "That bad?"

She shivered. "Yes."

I turned and ran down the hallway.

"Hey!" she shouted. "Get your ass back here!"

Nope, that wasn't happening. Thankfully, the room was close.

As I twisted the doorknob, Sierra caught up to me, but it was too late. The door swung open.

Blood coated the brown carpet and Alex's green shirt, but the most disturbing view wasn't the blood. It was Klyn, or what used to be Klyn.

His body was propped against the wall, but his head had been ripped off. If I'd ever wanted to know what the inside of someone's neck looked like, mission accomplished.

Muscle tissue hung in ways I didn't want to remember. And the worst part was that Klyn's head rested upside down beside him.

"Get her out of here!" Alex yelled at Sierra. "What the hell?"

"She ran away!" Sierra yelled back.

Vomit shot up my throat, and I stumbled toward the half bath down the hall.

I nearly didn't make it in time. As I hit my knees in front of the toilet, the vomit spewed.

I emptied my stomach over and over again. Each time I thought I was done, the image would pop back into my brain and the entire process would start again.

"You were supposed to keep her out of there," Alex hissed. "I warned you she was hardheaded." His footsteps drew closer, and the faucet turned on.

"She moved faster than I expected," Sierra justified. "I thought if she did something stupid, I could catch her."

His signature scent hit my nose as a damp, cool washcloth was pressed against my forehead. Between the sweet smell and the washcloth, my stomach eased enough to give me a glimmer of hope that I wouldn't need to keep hugging the toilet.

"Hold this," Alex said gently. "I'll go grab another one to put on the back of your neck."

I'd never had someone take care of me like this, not even Eliza. Granted, I hardly ever got sick. "Okay." I couldn't protest even if I'd wanted to.

Within seconds, another cool washcloth was pressed against the back of my neck, and more of my nausea subsided. "I'm okay." I didn't want him hovering over me. I despised that he was seeing me this way. If he hadn't thought I was weak before, he had to now.

Something thumped down the hall, and I glanced over my shoulder. Alex blocked my line of sight.

"Don't look," he said gently. "It's best if you don't."

"You couldn't have let us take him outside first?" Griffin grumbled.

Killian groaned. "Come help us out now that Ronnie isn't spewing anymore."

"Ew," Sierra whined. "Now I may spew because of what you said."

"That's worse than hearing and smelling it?" Rosemary asked. She sounded so confused, that if I'd felt better, I would've laughed.

"Yes, because I didn't see her do it." Sierra sighed dramatically. "But *spew* puts a certain visual in my head that I can't unsee." She gagged.

I could relate. Each time I closed my eyes, the image of

Klyn's headless body leapt into my brain. It would be a long time before I could close my eyes without seeing that image.

Many sleepless nights loomed ahead of me.

"I should help them." Alex placed his hand on my shoulder. "Will you be okay here for a few minutes?"

Sierra stomped her foot. "Uh ... I'm *right* here."

Alex didn't miss a beat. "That didn't prevent this from happening, so you should understand why I'm not comforted by that."

"Listen here, blood addict." Sierra's voice grew louder.

"Let's stop fighting," Sterlyn interjected, "and deal with this mess. The sooner we clean it up, the quicker Ronnie will rebound."

That got Alex in gear. "You're right. Sierra, yell if she needs me."

"Does it only have to be if she needs you? Because I'm fine yelling at you for fun." Sierra reached past me and flushed the toilet. "Oh, dear God. Don't you know if it's not yellow, flush it down?"

I snorted, and some of the acid burned the inside of my nose. "Oh, damn. Don't make me laugh. But you are aware you butchered that saying."

"Whatever." She waved her hand in front of her nose. "All I know is we need to get the smell off you and out of this bathroom."

I forced myself to focus. "I need a change of clothes, but I really don't want to go in that room." I climbed to my feet and removed the washcloths from my forehead and neck.

Sierra nodded. "I'll go get them and meet you in the room across the hall."

That sounded perfect, so I took a moment to brush my teeth and rid myself of the nastiness, rinsing my mouth before heading out the door.

With each step, my legs grew stronger. The door on the right from this direction came before the one on the left, so I wouldn't be tempted to glance in that room.

This bedroom had the same style of furniture as the one I'd been staying in, but instead of a walk-in closet, this closet had a simple sliding door, and the room was a little smaller, meaning there was still plenty of room for me.

My room back home was half the size, and I could only fit a full bed in it. This room was big enough for the king-sized bed centered against one wall to have plenty of walking room around it.

As I wiped my face with another washcloth, Sierra joined me with some gray yoga pants and a pale pink shirt. "Hope this is okay. You didn't have many clothes to choose from."

"It's fine. Thanks." I tossed the washcloth onto the dresser and took the clothes from her. "Do you mind shutting the door?" I didn't mind changing in front of her, but I didn't want Alex, Griffin, or Killian to walk by and get a peek.

She shut the door, and I changed.

"Yeah, I only bought a couple of outfits," I explained. "I didn't expect to be here so long."

"If I were you, I'd do another run and get a *lot* more outfits." She sat on the bed and stretched.

"Why? I shouldn't be here much longer." As soon as we resolved this situation, I had to go home.

Sierra fell back onto the bed and looked up at me. "I hate to tell you this, but there's no way you're leaving here permanently."

"Why would you say that?" I avoided her gaze as I paced the room to release some of the nervous energy bubbling inside me. The sounds of cleaning and footsteps going back and forth between the bedroom and outside had me on edge. One bright spot was that the smell of chemicals now covered the metallic stench of Klyn's blood.

Rolling her eyes, Sierra scoffed. "First, do you think there is any way in hell you're getting rid of me?" She wagged a finger at me. "Nope, not happening. I'll hunt you down if I have to." She pointed at her nose. "I'm a good tracker and have an excellent sense of smell."

"What?" I forced my mouth to drop. "You do? You could've fooled me."

She grabbed a pillow and threw it at me.

I dodged that one, but she countered by throwing another at me. The second one hit me in the side.

"Ouch!" I groaned and clutched my side. "How could you?"

The door to the room flew open, and Alex rushed in. His teeth extended as he glared at Sierra and hissed, "What did you do to her?"

Tense energy crackled through the room, and I blinked before understanding kicked in. "I was kidding." I snatched the two pillows from the floor. "She tossed pillows at me, and I tried channeling her personality with the dramatics."

"Hey!" Sierra snorted then broke into laughter. "I should be the one who's mad right now."

Alex exhaled and glanced from the pillows in my hands to Sierra. "But you said *ouch*."

"And for the record," Sierra said as she sat upright and pointed at Alex, "*that's* reason two."

"Why am I second?" His teeth shrank back to normal size, and he scratched his head.

She opened her mouth, and I wanted to kick her ass. "You're not number two."

"You know, you're right." She arched her brow and smirked. "He's reason one, but dammit, I should be."

Alex rubbed his temples. "I'm lost. You're not hurt?"

"Well, I don't know, Alex." Sierra lifted another pillow. "These things are kinda hard." She launched it at him. "She might not be able to walk for a while. Maybe you should give her some of your blood to heal up."

"Don't be a bitch," he said with that cocky smile that made my stomach flutter.

Sierra threw her hands up. "And there's the dog joke. I was wondering how long it'd take you to work yourself up to that."

"All right." Sterlyn clapped her hands as she joined us in the room. "It's all cleaned up. I hope nothing like that ever happens in our house again." She cut her gaze to Alex. "Understood?"

"He had to die, and I couldn't chance taking him outside, in case he got loose and attacked Veronica," Alex said as he strolled over to me.

Griffin stepped into the doorway with a frown. "Now we have to inform the council about this. A vampire dying in our home won't go over well."

"It'll be fine." Alex inched closer. "I'll tell them I killed him. They can't argue against me since he was one of my people."

Oh, right. He was the *prince*. "You guys keep talking about a council. You told me a little earlier, but I'm still not sure what that means? Your cities are separate, but all the supernaturals are allowed on this side of the river and not the other."

"Shadow Ridge and Shadow Terrace were founded to protect Shadow City." Sterlyn ran her hands over her jeans. "That's where Rosemary, Alex, and Griffin grew up."

"But not you, Killian, and Sierra?" The more puzzle pieces I got, the more confused I became. "And where is Shadow City?"

Rosemary marched into the room and placed her hands on her hips. "I get we all like Ronnie, but we have to remember she is *human*. Telling her more puts her in danger."

"She's right." Alex nodded. "She's in enough danger."

I despised not knowing. "But—"

"I'm sorry, but they're right." Sterlyn sighed, walked over, and patted my shoulder. "It's late. We all need to get some rest."

No, I wasn't ready. I wanted more answers, and as soon as I was alone, I wouldn't be able to stop myself from thinking about Klyn. I rubbed my arms, trying to stay warm and calm.

"I'm not leaving," Alex said softly, crossing his arms.

Griffin growled, "There's no way in hell that you're staying here."

CHAPTER SEVENTEEN

Alex and Griffin glared at each other in a battle of wills.

"I wasn't asking for permission," Alex said. "You couldn't protect her, so I have to stay."

"This is my house." Griffin took a menacing step toward us. "You need my permission, and it's not granted, so get your ass out."

If someone didn't intervene, this would go bad. I touched Alex's arm and tried to reason with him. "He's right. This is his house. If he doesn't want you here—"

"There's no way I'm leaving you again." Alex flexed his fingers. "And if they're hesitant to kill anyone who comes after you, you're at risk with them."

If that was true, it didn't matter. "The other choice is for me to go to a hotel. Then I won't have any friends around. Although, anyone coming after me might not be able to find me so easily. Do you think someone else might attack me?"

"Yes." Alex cracked his knuckles. "The reason I didn't want you to find Annie with me is because you're more likely to get hurt when you're around more vampires. When you strutted in there after me, throwing a tantrum ... every person in the bar became interested in you. That's why I kissed you that way in front of everyone, but it also put a bigger target on your back because of the civil unrest that's going on. They want to find a weakness in my family, and they see you as a bargaining chip, especially since I wanted you enough to make everyone aware of my interest."

"So you peed on her." Sierra laughed. "Here you are, making dog jokes, yet you marked your territory."

"And you say I misread social situations." Rosemary shook her head. "Now isn't the time for jokes."

"If it made me more of a target, why did you do it?" The missing piece wasn't clicking. I understood that Klyn and Eilam wanted to lose their humanity, and the royal family stood in their way, and that being with me wasn't an option for Alex because I was human. So why had he claimed me? And why continue to protect me? It'd have been easier if they'd killed me.

"Because if I hadn't, one of those assholes would've attacked you." He placed a fist on his mouth. "I did it to save you, and I didn't think they'd be stupid enough to attack you here, in shifter territory. I was wrong, and I'm kicking myself over it."

"You mean with all of them?" They were all wolf shifters, other than Rosemary.

"No, Sterlyn is a special type of wolf." Alex pointed at her. "And I knew Rosemary visited here often. I thought you would be safe, but I was wrong."

"A special type of wolf?" Her hair and skin did glow outside. Maybe that had something to do with it. "What do you mean?"

"I'm part angel, so my wolf is stronger than a typical shifter." Sterlyn moved to stand between the two fighting males. "And it's clear Alex won't leave Ronnie's side, and her going to a hotel is not an option."

I expected an outburst from Griffin, but the room went quiet. I gazed between the two, who were having one of those nonverbal conversations.

"A hotel is fine." I should have insisted that Alex leave, but I didn't want to acknowledge that I wanted him with me. He made me feel safe.

"No, it's not. That just puts you around others I don't trust." Alex exhaled and looked squarely at Griffin. "I know we haven't gotten along. I'm partly to blame, but you haven't been the most welcoming either." He rolled his shoulders. "It's clear you all care for her, and so do I. I need to be here to make sure she doesn't get hurt, so I would appreciate it if you'd let me stay."

For him to hand them an olive branch meant way too much to me. He was doing it because he wanted to stay here with me. He and I were getting too involved, but I was tired of fighting it.

Griffin's head dropped, and he rubbed his mouth. "Fine. But it's only because Sterlyn is on the same page as you. One wrong move—"

"You've already told me this," Alex sniped. "Repeating the same threat diminishes its desired effect."

And things had been going so well.

Griffin thrust out his chest. "Maybe I should show you instead of saying it."

"As much as I appreciate you allowing him to stay," I interjected, trying to diffuse the situation, "I'm not thrilled about sleeping in that room." Needless to say, it also over-looked the backyard, which was how the vampire had gotten inside.

"That's an easy problem to solve." Sterlyn motioned to the bed in this room. "You can have this room instead."

"But sometimes, Rosemary and Sierra stay over." The house felt like a revolving door, but this group acted more like family than friends.

"Nope, I planned on sleeping in my own room for the next few nights." Sierra shuddered. "Apparently, I haven't been spending enough time at home."

Killian leaned against the doorframe. "Yet, here you are."

"Hey, I'll come hang out in the morning so they can bask in my presence." Sierra wrinkled her nose. "Don't give me lip. You may be my alpha, but others deserve the opportunity to be around me as well."

"Please, let them." Killian stuck out his tongue. "That way, when we watch our action movies, we won't have to hear you whine."

"Not cool." She bared her teeth at me playfully. "I still blame you for this."

Alex pursed his lips but remained quiet, watching our interaction.

"Don't listen to her." Rosemary closed her eyes. "We all know she can be a tad dramatic."

"Now listen—" Sierra started.

Rosemary cut her off. "And I didn't plan on staying over this week. Things are going down in Shadow City that I need to be there for during the day, so I'll go home too."

"It's settled." Sterlyn clapped. "There's no reason for you to go to a hotel."

"And if that changes..." Killian shrugged. "I have two extra bedrooms of my own right next door."

Since everyone was always here, I often forgot that Killian was their neighbor.

"Maybe Alex could stay with you, so he'll be close to Ronnie," Griffin suggested, driving the point home that he didn't want the vampire in his house.

I hated being the reason for the contention. "If that would make you more comfortable—"

"No, we're safer here." Alex grimaced. "Not that you"—he nodded to Killian—"aren't a good protector. It's just that the moon is getting fuller, and Sterlyn is here."

Every time I felt like I was catching up, they'd throw in a comment like that. "What does the moon have to do with Sterlyn?"

"Rosemary's uncle was the guardian of the moon, and he procreated with a wolf, which resulted in the silver wolves." Sterlyn gestured to her hair and eyes. "Our wolf side is more dominant, but our angel powers tie us to the moon. On a full moon, we're at our strongest, but on a new moon, our strength, size, and speed are like that of a regular wolf."

Wow. And the strangest part was that this sounded logical. That was how far I'd come in the last week. I'd learned to accept the unexpected, and that had helped my mental health.

"As exciting as this is, I'm heading out." Sierra yawned, covering her mouth. "Between working all day, the fake vampire attack that led to a real one, a dead body, and Ronnie yacking, I'm exhausted."

Killian winced. "Did you really need to repeat all that? We were there for it."

"You were not at Dick's Bar." She placed her hands on her hips. "Ugh, I mean Wolf Lounge. I'm not sure which name is worse."

Killian's neck stiffened. "You complained enough, so it felt like we were all there."

"Bite me." She lifted her chin in defiance.

"Um ..." Sterlyn chuckled. "Are you sure you should be saying that with a vampire nearby?"

"Hey," Alex snapped and winked at me. "I'm only interested in biting one person."

My heart picked up its pace, his words thrilling me. Him biting me didn't sound painful or like a punishment.

"Okay, ew." Sierra stood from the bed and marched to the door. "And that seals the deal. I'm outta here. See ya later, suckers." She made her way into the hallway and disappeared from sight. Within seconds, the front door opened and closed.

"And on that note." Rosemary huffed. "I should head out too. I'll fly over the woods to ensure nothing is out of the ordinary. Just text me if you need me, and I can be here quickly."

"Thanks." Killian pushed off from the doorframe. "A fly-over would be great. There are twenty guards on watch for the rest of the night, so we should be okay."

Rosemary gave one of her rare grins. "If anything seems weird, call me. I'll have my phone on me."

"Will do," Sterlyn said. "And having Alex here makes me more comfortable too. A vampire would have to go against their prince to harm her. That wouldn't be very smart."

"I'm sorry I'm putting all of you out." I felt worthless because I was so much weaker than them. I was lucky to have held off Klyn for as long as I had.

Sterlyn placed a hand on my shoulder and tilted my head so that I had to gaze into her eyes. She said softly, "You're not a burden. Don't ever feel that way. Each one of us loves and cares for you, and that's why we're protecting you."

Overwhelming emotions swirled inside me. "I care about you all as well." I couldn't say *I love you*. I'd never told anyone that, not even Eliza and Annie, and I loved them with my entire heart. But those words would make me so vulnerable, and I'd already broken so many of my own, personal rules with them.

"Okay, I'm heading out." Rosemary tugged at her maroon shirt. "See you later." She practically ran out of the house.

"Is she okay?" Her urgency to leave made me a little uncomfortable. "Did I do something?"

"No. Angels aren't known for being in tune with their feelings." Sterlyn snorted. "She was uncomfortable with our little display and wanted to get out, but she's better than she used to be."

"Is she, though?" Killian's voice rose with sarcasm.

"Leave her alone," Sterlyn chastised as she smacked his arm. "Are you heading out too?"

"Nah, I'm thinking I'll stay here and crash in the other bedroom."

"Oh, then stay in this room." Even though I didn't want to sleep where Klyn had attacked me, I hated making someone else do it.

"Death doesn't bother me." Killian stared at the floor. "So it's nothing at all."

"Before we go, I want to know what's going on with the vampires." Griffin crossed his arms. "Nothing has been brought to the council, and since we're allowing Alex to stay here, we deserve some answers."

Alex grunted. "You can kiss—"

I cut him off before the situation turned volatile again. "Griffin's right. Not only have they let me stay here, but they're also risking their lives for me. Now that I know about the supernatural world, I want to know as well." These two were so damn similar they couldn't stand each other.

"Fine," Alex bit out. "But this stays between the five of us."

"Like hell—" Griffin started, but Sterlyn lifted a hand.

"Babe, do we want to know or not?" Sterlyn challenged. "Let's be real. We've kept stuff from the council before too. I'm okay keeping it between us as long as no one is at risk."

"I'd like to know what's going on, too, since we're relying on the vampires to keep that side of Shadow City safe." Killian placed his hands on top of his head. "As long as you're fixing the problem, I'll keep my mouth shut—unless you don't get your shit figured out quick enough."

"We are working on it." Alex paced in front of the bed. "But while Shadow City was essentially locked down for so long, things got out of hand in Shadow Terrace."

"Like blatantly attacking humans out of hand?" Griffin growled.

Alex nodded. "Yes, but Matthew, Gwen, and I didn't realize how bad it was until Veronica came to town, searching for her sister. Vampire rebels have infiltrated Shadow Terrace and are integrating into Shadow Ridge University to funnel their desire for blood. Blade, the vampire who managed Shadow Terrace before the gates opened, was informing us about the rebellion at Thirsty's the night I met Veronica. At first, the group was small, but in the last month, their numbers have grown. These vampires target humans who don't have a strong parental base."

"Like Annie. She was part of the foster care system." Eliza had never formally adopted us because she couldn't afford the fees. Because both Annie's and my parents were out of the picture, we'd never had to worry about being rehomed, and now we were both of age.

"Exactly." Alex stopped pacing. "So we have Eilam drying out, not only to put Annie's mind back together, but also to tell us who is working with him."

My stomach dropped. "What if he doesn't give you names?" I didn't want Annie to be his puppet forever.

"As long as he fixes Annie's mind, we'll kill him and use him as an example for his followers." He exhaled. "That should scare them back into line. But Matthew and I are handling it. They aren't targeting tourists with families, just individuals."

I blinked, debating how much I cared that Alex was talking about outright execution so calmly.

I decided ... not much. These assholes deserved to die.

"But it's still not right." Sterlyn mashed her lips together. "That's risky. We don't need that kind of attention from the human realm. If too many people go missing—"

"We know." Alex groaned. "This group did something to get a massive jump in numbers so quickly, and I won't rest until we figure it out. Just give us some time."

"If things get worse, we'll have to go to the council." Griffin karate chopped the air.

I needed to help Alex, since they were all ganging up on him. "Is that why you were having so many meetings at Thirsty's?"

"Yeah, we're trying to uncover the members of the group." He smiled at me gratefully. "I have a feeling the bar owner has a hand in it, and we're shutting down the bar as we speak. He won't have access to blood until this is handled."

If they were trying to go under the radar with tourists,

they'd failed on that one. "The bar does have a dark, vampy feel."

"Had we known the place would be constructed that way, we wouldn't have approved it." Alex lifted a hand. "But that's what happens when city and building plans are passed through Shadow City without any transparency. Matthew and I are dedicated to eliminating the threat."

"And it looks like Ronnie and her sister are your keys." Killian frowned. "Which is unfortunate."

"But we're all protecting them, which is what matters." Sterlyn yawned. "We can talk about this more tomorrow. It's time to get some rest." She motioned for Alex to follow her. "Come on, I'll get some covers for the couch."

Alex stayed in place, refusing to budge. "I'm sleeping in here."

"No, you're not!" Being alone with him in this room was not a smart idea.

He stepped toward me and rasped, "There is no way you're getting me out of this room, Veronica. You might as well accept it."

Those words rubbed me wrong. I hated being told what to do.

I glared at him. "We'll see about that."

CHAPTER EIGHTEEN

"I feel like I'm watching the beginning of a porno," Killian whispered loud enough for me to hear.

And here I'd thought Sierra had the worst mouth among them. There was a ton of sexual tension between Alex and me, but I had hoped that no one else had picked up on that. "You need to shut it."

Griffin scowled at Alex as he said, "Which is more reason for him not to stay with us."

"There will be *no* sex," Alex said firmly. "This is purely about being near in case something slips past you three again."

Wow. Obviously, my feelings were one-sided because he sounded disgusted by the thought of sex with me.

"You're not helping." Sterlyn inhaled deeply then exhaled. "I vouched for you, then you go and throw insults at us like that. Either respect everyone here or leave. Now."

That was one thing I liked most about Sterlyn. She was direct, but not overly blunt like Rosemary. Sterlyn had an air of authority like no one I'd been around before. When she spoke, people wanted to listen.

"I didn't mean it as an insult." Alex shrugged with his usual cockiness. "I was merely stating facts. I'm sorry if you don't appreciate that."

Now I was hurt and pissed. "If it weren't for your failed ninja shenanigans, the vampire wouldn't have found me in the first place or snuck in because we would've all been here in the house. So if you're going to point a finger at anyone, it should be at *your* sorry ass."

Sterlyn nodded. "I couldn't have said it any better."

"Fine." Alex rubbed his chin and scoffed. "If you don't want me to stay in your room, no problem."

"I'll go grab you some blankets and pillows." Sterlyn spun on her heel and strolled out, leaving me alone with the three men.

None of them budged, their bodies tense. I wasn't supernatural, but even I could smell the testosterone in the air.

I was tempted to follow Sterlyn, but I didn't want their blood on my hands. It was clear they didn't get along, but I wasn't sure if they just didn't like each other or if it was more of a race thing. "I hope I'm not the reason you all stopped getting along."

Alex snorted, but his body didn't relax. "Don't flatter yourself." His fingers twitched as if he thought Killian and Griffin might attack. "This isn't about you."

That was the second snide remark he'd thrown my way in less than five minutes. I refused to be someone's punching bag. "You're a jackass."

His head jerked in my direction, and his nostrils flared. "Do you know how much I've sacrificed for you?"

"What?" That wasn't the reaction I'd been hoping for.

"Oh, please." Griffin's laughter had an edge. "Don't

manipulate her. Vampires don't do anything unless there's something in it for them."

"And what am I gaining by protecting her?" Alex asked as he shook a fist at me. "Causing problems between Matthew and me? Sneaking around behind not only my people's backs but yours? Please, enlighten me."

"She's your bait." Killian planted his feet wide apart. "You're using her to weed out vampires who aren't obeying the council's orders. You already admitted you don't want the council to know what these rogue vampires are doing, and she's the best way to draw them out."

Damn. I hadn't considered that. Maybe he was using my feelings to his advantage. I'd thought he was struggling the same way I was, but Killian had a point.

God, I'd been so stupid. Here I was, drooling over him. I searched for anger, but all I felt was heartbreak. Once again, another person had manipulated me to benefit themselves.

"You *prick*." A vein bulged in Alex's neck. "Don't sit there and act like you know what my intent is or what my feelings are for her."

I shouldn't have been surprised that he'd deflect instead of addressing the accusation head-on. That solidified everything. "How he feels about me doesn't matter. If he wants to use me to weed out the rogues who are doing this to Annie and who knows how many others, I'm okay with it. As long as Annie is freed, I'll do whatever it takes." I hoped the sob choking me wasn't obvious.

Alex winced. "That's—"

Sterlyn entered the room, carrying two pillows and a blanket. "No matter how we feel, Ronnie has a right to do whatever she wants, just like I did when I arrived here. We respect her decision, and we'll do everything we can to protect her."

Her understanding didn't surprise me. She and I were on the same wavelength, and I was certainly glad she had my back. Killian and Griffin wouldn't push as hard to get rid of me since Sterlyn was on my side.

"You're right." Griffin's body loosened. "And we do need to get the vampires in line. They can't protect that side of the river if they're too focused on feeding and disobeying orders."

We needed to disperse before they began arguing again. I forced a yawn and stretched. "Guys, it's midnight, and I'm exhausted."

"Me, too." Sterlyn lifted the blanket and pillows. "Come on, Alex, let's get you set up."

He ran his fingers through his hair and nibbled on his bottom lip, staying put.

If he was going to insist on staying in this room with me again, I might lose it. After this entire conversation, he should know better. Maybe he was messing with my mind by making me think he couldn't alter my thoughts. Ugh, maybe I was as bad off as Annie, and he'd left me more self-aware, so Sterlyn and the others would think he was on their side. "You heard her," I said clearly, making sure he realized there was no doubt. "Head into the living room. I don't want you in here with me." That had sounded harsh. And even though I shouldn't have cared, I did, so I added, "I want to be alone."

His gaze flicked over me, searching for something.

"Come on." Killian rocked on his heels. "She's not lying. We all know that. If she doesn't want us in here, we're going to respect her wishes."

"Fine." Alex huffed, but he still didn't budge.

What the hell was he doing? Despite knowing better, I met his eyes.

Yup, I shouldn't have. His eyes told so many stories, but the concern etched into his face almost softened me toward him again.

No, Ronnie. Don't fall for it. I would not be under someone's spell. I was my own damn person, and that couldn't change.

Not for anybody.

I schooled my expression, not wanting him to see the hurt and turmoil underneath. Even though my heart felt shattered, I'd never let him know that he had that much of an effect on me.

"Come on, Alex." Sterlyn headed back into the hallway. "Let's get you settled."

He cleared his throat as if to capture my attention again, but I focused on Sterlyn's retreating figure. I didn't want to chance him seeing through my act. My feelings slipped through the longer we were together.

After a moment, he gave up and followed Sterlyn without another glance my way.

Distance between us was for the best. I had to remember that.

Griffin stepped up to me and lowered his voice. "If anything happens that you're uncomfortable with, just yell."

Tears pricked my eyes, and I smiled at him. He'd been so standoffish with me that his concern and protective attitude caught me off guard. I'd noticed that he wasn't glaring or scowling at me as much, but this was the first direct proof that he cared. "Okay. Thank you." I wasn't sure what else to say.

In general, I wasn't comfortable expressing my emotions. When I felt too much, I tended to shut down. Like now. When someone knew how much they could affect you, they had too much control over you. Even with Eliza and Annie, I sometimes remained aloof, but they knew me so well that they realized whenever I acted that way, it was because I felt too much. In a way, it was me saying I love you.

"And I'm right across the hall." Killian waggled his eyebrows at me. "In the death room, so don't call for help from me."

A smile broke through without permission. He was the second likeliest person to make me laugh, and I both enjoyed and hated it. Sierra was the first. She and Killian were similar, but Sierra was way more outspoken. Killian had more of a filter, though it failed him on occasion.

"Oh, then I'll definitely be screaming for you." I stopped, realizing how that statement could be taken. My face heated, and I hoped my mind was the only one in the gutter.

"Well now." Griffin chuckled. "Please don't scream it loud enough that we all hear what's happening on this side of the house."

And there it was. My mind had company.

"That's not what I meant." I didn't want Killian to think I was hitting on him. That could make this whole friendship thing awkward, and I didn't want to lose that with them. "Not that you aren't attractive. You are." I'd never had problems with a loose tongue until I'd arrived here. I didn't know if it was because I was that comfortable with them or that intimidated. "You're one of the top five hottest guys I've ever seen." And now it sounded like I was hitting on him again.

"Top five?" He frowned, even though his chocolate eyes warmed. "Not number one?"

Unfortunately, Alex held the number one spot. Stupid

vampire. But I didn't want to hurt his feelings. "Yup, sure, number one."

Griffin laughed so hard it startled me. He waved his hand in front of his nose and barely got out, "Oh, sorry, man. You are definitely not number one."

Now my face was on fire. I'd forgotten they could smell a lie. From what Sterlyn had told me, it smelled like rotten eggs. "I was trying to be nice." I closed my eyes, praying they would disappear.

"On that note, I need to go lick my wounds." Kilian winked at me. "Good night. But seriously, I'll be here if you need me."

"Thank you." I wished more than anything I could tell him not to worry, that I could handle it on my own, but I couldn't. That was one lesson Eliza had taught me shortly after I'd moved in with her. It wasn't weak to ask for help when you needed it. And boy, did I need it now.

"Good night," Griffin said as he also walked out the door.

Not wanting to chance Alex coming back in here alone, I rushed to the door to shut and lock it. With that settled, I faced the room and laid the back of my head against the door. All the emotions I'd been holding back flooded through me, and I struggled to breathe.

I slid down to the floor onto my ass and cried silently. I felt alone and petrified. If only Annie hadn't come to visit the college, we would be safe back at home. Annie wouldn't be in danger, and I wouldn't have met all these people I clicked with—or who had scared me to death.

In other words, things would be easier. Sometimes, it was best not to know what you were missing.

As much as it hurt to think about leaving, I was also scared to stay. I was human, and everyone around me was stronger, faster, and—hell, I had to be real—smarter. They knew how this world worked, whereas I was barely treading water. If leaving this behind kept Annie safe, I'd make that sacrifice, even if my heart would never be whole again.

Sometimes, family was more important than yourself.

A light knock on the door startled me. I glanced at the clock and saw that I'd been drowning in my emotions for over fifteen minutes.

Alex's smooth, deep voice whispered, "Veronica, may I please talk to you for a minute?"

"No." I'd locked the door because of him. Letting him inside would defeat that purpose. "Leave me alone." Hurt broke through my words, infuriating me. I didn't want him to know.

"Earlier, there was a huge misunderstanding." There was a bump on the door like he'd knocked his forehead against it. "Give me a chance to explain. Please."

If I let him in, I'd be tempted to let him stay. "No, I think you were very clear. There's no need to rehash it."

"That's the thing. I want to say more now that we're alone." He sounded flustered. "I couldn't, not with everyone around. There's so much that needs to be said. Please, let me in."

My heart yelled at me to do it. His request was so damn tempting. And that was why I couldn't. He wanted to explain why he didn't want me, and he didn't have to. I understood all too clearly. He was a prince, a vampire, and he'd been afraid that if he'd been honest with me, I wouldn't have willingly acted as his bait.

I would've been more than happy. No one deserved to have their mind messed with the way Annie's had been. "I need you to leave me alone."

"Dammit, Veronica," Alex growled. "Are you really

going to make me say this through the door? Because you're going to hear what I have to say one way or another."

The door across the hall opened, and Killian said threateningly, "You heard her. She doesn't want to talk to you. Why don't you leave her alone?"

"Because I need to talk with her ... alone," Alex said with frustration.

Oh, great. This was going to go bad if I didn't step in. I didn't have it in me to deal with yet another fight.

I opened the door and glared at the vampire. "Let's get this over with."

CHAPTER NINETEEN

"See, she invited me in," Alex gloated as his cocky grin appeared. "Thanks for the assist."

Killian glowered and gripped the doorknob. "Remember. You don't have to do anything you don't want to."

How I wished I didn't want to be near Alex, but I did. Self-preservation was hard to maintain around him. That was why I hadn't let him in to begin with. We had a connection that was so strong the intensity stole my breath.

And I wasn't being dramatic.

Sometimes, I couldn't function around him. "He's determined to have his say, so it's easier to let him get it out so I can go to bed."

"Aw, my dear, sweet mother always said that someday my persistence would pay off." Alex winked and slipped by me into the bedroom.

I swallowed my smile, not wanting to encourage the vampire more. Right now, I had a concerned friend who needed my reassurance.

"Is this wise?" Killian asked as he glanced over my

shoulder. "He's been protecting you, but we don't know why."

"If I need you, I'll holler." And people said women were dramatic. These men fought and snapped at each other more than any group of girls I'd ever met. "Let me hear him out." I was so damn tired, and if they didn't stop, I might let them go at each other. Maybe it would resolve whatever supernatural drama was simmering between them.

Killian groaned. "If he so much as touches your arm without your approval, I will kick his ass. You're like a sister to me," Killian murmured. "And I protect those I love."

I believed him. "I feel the same way about all of you."

"As touching as this is," Alex interrupted, standing beside me, "I was the one who requested a conversation with Veronica, not you."

Killian tapped his foot and crossed his arms. "Are you sure you want to talk to this asshole?"

"It's fine." My eyes grew heavier. "I'll let you know if I need you."

He hesitated, and I thought he was going to say something else, but he walked back into his room, leaving his door wide open.

The message was clear: He was ready to react if something horrible went down.

I faced Alex, expecting him to be annoyed, but he stood as still as a statue.

"Are you okay?" Something was off. He was never quiet and enjoyed being the center of attention.

"Yeah, it's just peculiar," he stated as he shut the door. I heard the lock click; then he turned to me. "I brought you here for them to protect you, but I didn't expect you to become friends."

"Is that a problem?" If anything, them caring about me

made them more invested in my safety, but he didn't seem happy about it.

He placed his hands behind his back. "No, not necessarily. It's just they don't like me."

"So ... because they don't like you, they shouldn't like me?" For once, he wasn't being cocky. He was truly perplexed. "We aren't a package deal."

His head jerked up, and his soft blue eyes locked with mine. "But aren't we?"

My stomach fluttered, and no matter how hard I tried to squash the sensation, it wouldn't stop. "I'm not in the mood for mind games." I took a second to remind myself that he had the ability to mess with me. My feelings might not be real.

"In a way, I wish this was a game." His shoulders sagged as he exhaled. "It would make things so much easier."

"What would be easier?" He was speaking in riddles, and I didn't have the patience for it.

"Tonight, when Sterlyn informed me that you'd been attacked, it changed ... everything." He licked his lips.

Something inside me responded to his words as if I understood where he was going, but my brain hadn't caught up yet. "Are—" My voice cracked, cutting me off. "Are you tired of me?"

He laughed without humor. "No, not at all."

"Then what changed?" My legs were frozen in place and sweat coated my palms. I wasn't sure whether I should run to him or away from him.

"I'm not willing to let you go. Not any longer." He watched me with such intensity. "I'm tired of fighting our bond."

"You feel it too?" I heard the words, but they weren't making sense. I'd thought the connection between us was a figment of my imagination—the stuff movies were made of. "And what do you mean by *let me go*? You said we couldn't be together since I'm human."

"That first night you appeared in Shadow Terrace, I was upstairs in the bar's meeting room. Blade and I were talking about the rogue group in there so we could keep an eye on the bar's owner, but then something snapped inside my chest." He wrung his hands together. "I tried to ignore it, but the *yanking* grew stronger until I had to figure out what it was. I walked downstairs, and saw you walk through the door."

I remembered that night vividly. The darkness inside the bar had made it so hard to see, and unease had coiled inside me.

"My world shifted, then that bastard shoved you against the wall with the sole intent to feed," he spat, his body shaking with rage. "He was so driven by bloodlust that he didn't see me standing there. The more a vampire drinks from a human to the point of death or hurts them out of pure enjoyment, the more of their humanity they lose. It can be gradual or fast, depending on how fast the vampire becomes addicted to it. You can tell who has lost all their humanity because they can't even stand being in the moonlight unless they're fully clothed. Fortunately, my family and I are stronger than most because we are from the original bloodline. If we were to cave to our baser instincts, it would be detrimental to the entire vampire population. When Klyn attacked you that night and nearly bit you tonight, I had to end him. I had no choice."

A chill ran through me. I hadn't needed to be supernatural to feel the weird vibes from Klyn. "Oh, I was there. You don't have to remind me." Talking about it made the attack surge to the forefront of my mind. "But I'd rather not talk about that. Not tonight."

"Ugh." He leaned his head back and inspected the white ceiling. "See, I keep messing this up. I've never had a problem talking to anyone until you."

"If you're going to start insulting me—"

"Just hear me out." His face softened, and he placed his hands together as if to pray.

How could I say no to that? "Go on." My legs were getting wobbly, and I wasn't sure how much longer I could stand here but sitting on the bed wouldn't be smart with him so close.

"At first, I didn't understand." He chuckled. "I mean, you're gorgeous, tenacious, and so damn stubborn that you drive me crazy, but you're human! But during the past week, I've done some digging into why I could possibly feel this connected to you, and everything clicked."

I wanted to yell at him to get to the point, but he was struggling with what to say. "What clicked?"

"You see, vampires have their humanity when they're born." He touched his chest. "And luckily, I haven't lost mine, or else I never would've felt *this*."

My pulse pounded in my ears, and I leaned forward in anticipation. Maybe I shouldn't have been this eager. He might say something I didn't want to hear, something he couldn't take back. Whatever his next words were, they would change my life.

"What I'm saying is ... you're my soulmate." He slowly walked over to me. "And I'm done fighting it. I'm all in if you'll have me."

"Soulmate?" I stared at him, waiting for him to laugh, but he didn't. And the term resonated deep within me. I could *feel* him each time he was close. That wasn't normal, but if we were two halves of the same soul, that made better sense.

But soulmates weren't real.

Then again, neither were supernaturals, and we all saw how well that "truth" had turned out.

He held my gaze steadily as my head swirled.

"That's crazy." But as I tried not to believe him, my desperate need to be with him and the way his scent and taste were my two favorite things in the world ... "What does that mean—*soulmate?*"

He stepped back, giving me space as he murmured, "In humans, the tug isn't as strong, so it's harder to discern it, other than feeling as if you've known each other your entire life. But with supernaturals, because we're part magic, the connection feels like a tug, a buzz, a yank, or some variation that pulls you together. It's our magic helping us identify our perfect match. And you're mine."

"But I'm *human.*" I grimaced and looked away. He'd poured out his heart, and I'd stated the obvious. "And I feel a yank or tug toward you, too."

"You do?" He sighed and relaxed. "It's probably because I'm supernatural and your soulmate. Maybe my magic yanks at you more."

"What does this mean?" My mind ran amuck. *Soulmate* sounded so deep and final. I'd never even had a boyfriend. Although Annie had always said I was an extremist, so why should this be any different? Why bother with a boyfriend when I could find the one person who could both destroy or make me whole?

"At first, I was determined to let you go." Alex bit his lower lip. "No matter whether you wanted to stay or not. But now ..." He closed the distance between us, and his scent made my head spin.

I tilted my head upward as our gazes met. Unable to stop myself, I placed my hands on his chest. He wasn't muscular like Killian but rather leaner and cut. I very much preferred the way he felt. "And now?"

"If you want to stay, I won't stop you," he rasped, his focus on my lips.

My body betrayed me as I inched closer to him. "And if I leave?"

His answer to this question was the most important one.

"After coming close to losing you tonight, I'll follow you wherever you go," he vowed and laid his forehead against mine. "I'm at your mercy. What we have is more important than anything, and I hope and pray you feel the same way about me."

"But you said my humanity would cause issues for you and your family." After losing my family and going without one for years, I never wanted to rip one apart. "I can't ..."

"You being human does make our connection problematic." He lifted his hands. "But I don't give a damn. Matthew and I vowed, when we were younger, that we wouldn't marry until we found the same love our parents had. They were the last soulmates of our kind in Shadow City, and we saw the devotion they had for each other. I'd never been seriously interested in any woman, so for you to come here and capture my heart speaks more than you'll ever know."

"But you said it would weaken your family's position in the vampire world." I didn't understand how royalty worked in this world, but I understood how it did in the human one.

"I'm just the spare, not the king." Determination hardened Alex's face. "And I'll walk away if it's the only way I can be with you. Gwen can take my place, even though Matthew will have a fit. Mom and Dad told me to always support Matthew, and if being with you means I need to step down to fulfill that promise by putting Gwen next in line, I'll do it in a heartbeat. I'd rather step away from my royal duties than lose you."

I smiled as every ounce of my defenses crumbled. It didn't make sense, yet it made the most sense in the world. I felt the same way about him and knowing I wouldn't have to live without him made my decision much easier. "I'm all yours." Unable to restrain myself any longer, I kissed him. His sweet taste was too damn addictive. I slipped my tongue inside his mouth, needing more.

His hands snaked around my waist and pulled me against his chest. He met each stroke of my tongue.

In his arms, I felt safer than ever before. After his vulnerable confession, I'd always want to be with him. The thought would've petrified me an hour ago, but something had truly changed between us.

He carried me to the bed and placed me gently on the mattress, his mouth still fused to mine. Everything around me blurred, and I closed my eyes, focusing on the sensations he aroused in me.

No one had ever made me feel this way, and I couldn't live without him either.

He pulled his mouth from mine and rained kisses down my face and neck. Maybe I should've been petrified, but the fear never manifested. His teeth raked my skin, but he didn't nick me.

I *wanted* him to drink from me, no matter how dangerous and irrational that might be. I grabbed his head to force him to bite me.

"Veronica," he groaned. "Don't tempt me. You smell delicious. It's hard enough to stay in control."

"Would it take away your humanity?" I asked. The last thing I wanted was for him to damn his soul.

He sniffed me. "Not if I drink from my soulmate, but—"

"Do it," I whispered as I writhed against him. I didn't know why, but I *needed* him to bite me.

"But—" he growled again. When he tried to pull away, I held on and whimpered, "Please."

"If I hurt you ..." he started, conflicting emotions heavy in his tone.

"I'll smack you," I promised.

His teeth raked my neck again, then something sharp pierced my skin. As soon as the burn began, it was gone, and my body warmed. I wrapped my legs around his waist, rubbing against him. The pressure built as he drank and slipped a hand under my shirt.

As his fingers gently caressed one breast and pinched my nipple, I moaned in pure ecstasy. I'd never imagined I could feel this turned on. On a high, I unbuttoned his pants and reached inside his boxers. He gasped and removed his teeth from my neck.

I almost cried in protest, but he licked where he'd bitten and kissed his way lower. He whispered, "God, you're so beautiful." He removed my shirt and bra, and his mouth teased my breasts as I stroked him.

Even though I had no clue what I was doing, his groans and murmurs empowered me. All my hesitancy fell away. Only we mattered, and nothing would change that. As much as I was his, he belonged to me. And we were both desperate to let the other person feel that.

He removed his mouth from my nipple and whispered, "You taste and smell amazing." His hand trailed down my stomach and slid underneath my yoga pants and between my legs. His fingers circled my core, and a sensation and pressure like I'd never felt before flooded my body.

I moaned as he slipped a finger inside me.

"You're a virgin?" he gasped, his voice thick with need.

Any other moment, I'd have been embarrassed, but I was riding high on these new feelings. "Yes."

"Damn, that's sexy," he hissed with approval. He slid in and out of me then added another finger.

Desperation climbed inside me as his mouth and fingers worked their magic. The pressure was building, and I needed to be fully satisfied. "Please, make love to me."

He exhaled. "We don't—"

"Now," I begged. "I want you."

"Are you sure?" he asked tentatively. "This will seal our fate. I mean—"

I kissed his lips, wanting him to shut up, and nodded. "More than anything."

He untangled from me and removed the rest of my clothing. When he was done, he stripped before me, staring at me the whole time as if he'd just received the best gift of his life. My eyes drank in his naked form, and I somehow grew even warmer. I wasn't even sure how.

Slowly, he climbed over me, shifting to rest between my legs. "You're sure?"

Instead of answering, I pulled his body closer to mine. With care, he inched inside me, letting me adjust before going deeper. I thought fleetingly of what an arrogant ass he'd been the day I met him. This proved he was so much more than that. He was made for me.

Once he was completely inside, he stilled until I nodded. Then he began to thrust, gently at first, his pace gradually increasing.

The feel of him made the friction build until I was

urging him to move faster. He grabbed my hands and locked them above my head as he slammed into me.

An orgasm rocked through me as he groaned in pleasure. Something *snapped* between us.

I love you, his voice said in my head, bringing me down from the moment.

"What the hell?" I said loudly.

"What's wrong?" Alex climbed off me, searching the room for what had scared me.

"I heard—" I started, but something thudded against the bedroom door.

CHAPTER TWENTY

I froze as Alex jumped off the bed and blurred, dressing within seconds.

Killian growled, "If you don't let me in, I will tear this fucking door down."

"Give us a second," Alex said with annoyance as he snatched my clothes from the floor and tossed them to me. "Hurry. He better not come in here and see you like this."

"Like what?" Killian bellowed. "What did you do to her?"

This whole situation had turned from the best dream I'd ever had into a nightmare, but I was on the same page as Alex. I didn't want Killian to see me in my birthday suit. I grabbed the shirt and yoga pants and threw them on as fast as humanly possible.

Even in this dire situation, the humor of my last thought didn't escape me.

Killian's voice lowered to a threatening level. "I swear, if you've done something to her, you won't have any teeth left to use for feeding."

My body warmed. When Alex had drunk from me, I'd

enjoyed it a little too much. But now wasn't the time for dirty thoughts. "He didn't do anything."

"I find that hard to believe." Killian banged on the door again. "Otherwise, this door would be open by now."

Two sets of footsteps ran down the hall toward our room.

Great, now everyone was up and raring to go again.

Sterlyn's voice rang out, strong and clear. "What's going on?"

"I don't know. I can smell sex, and Ronnie sounded scared. I'm trying to check on her, but the damn door is locked, and they won't let me in." Killian spoke so softly I almost couldn't hear him.

After the sex comment, I didn't want to face them. They already knew we'd had sex. How was I supposed to explain that without sounding crazy? I wanted to crawl back into bed and throw the covers over my head, but Killian and the others would bust in. I hurried to the door.

"It'll be fine," Alex assured me. "They'll understand."

Unease filtered through me, and I stopped short of the door. "What are you talking about?" It was like he knew what I was thinking, but that was impossible.

Please open the door before they kill me. He took a few steps away from the door. *I'll explain everything after that.*

As I touched the doorknob, concern washed over me, mixing with my own anxiety. I had to be losing it because I knew those words and concern had come from Alex. But how the hell was I hearing him in my mind and feeling his emotions? None of that was possible.

"Time's up," Killian rasped. "I'm tearing the door down."

"Dude," Griffin huffed. "There's a key on the top ledge

of the door frame just like in your house. You don't have to break the door."

Forcing myself to move, I unlocked the door and opened it to find all three of them standing in the hallway.

Sterlyn's face was lined with concern. "Are you—"

Oh shit. I'd forgotten about my neck. I placed my hand over where he'd bitten me, hoping no one else would see.

"Wait." Griffin's nostrils flared. "How the hell is this possible?"

"I made him do it." I wouldn't let Alex take the fall for this, especially since he'd refused at first. "It's not his fault."

"He told you that you were fated mates and that sex would complete the bond?" Sterlyn asked as her gaze flicked from him to me.

So this wasn't about him biting me. Whew. I needed to keep their attention diverted because I wasn't sure how they'd react if they knew. "Fated mates? Is that like soulmates?"

"You *asshole*," Killian growled as he rushed past me and punched Alex in the face. "You sealed the deal without telling her?"

"Fuck!" Alex hissed, rubbing his face. His fangs descended, and his irises turned red. "I get that you're protecting her, but if you punch me again, we'll have a serious problem."

"Hey!" I didn't know what was going on, but I hated that they were taking everything out on Alex. "I'm an adult, and I allowed this to happen. I asked for it. So if you're going to punch him, then you have to punch me too."

"He didn't tell you what you're getting into," Griffin growled, and his hands clenched into fists. "If Killian doesn't want to punch him again, I have no problem doing it myself."

I had no clue how to defuse the situation. I looked at Sterlyn, hoping she would help. She didn't seem angry, but she wasn't trying to calm them down. She was watching me.

Since she seemed rational, I'd appeal to her. "He told me we're soulmates. I'm thinking that's the same thing as fated mates, right?"

"Yeah, it is." She opened her mouth and closed it again, at a loss for words.

"Then he did tell me." I spun around and caught a glimpse of myself in the mirror. My hair was disheveled, and my lips were swollen. They'd have known what we'd done just by observing me. But the strangest part was that there was no bite mark on my neck. Alex must have healed it.

"And you're okay with it?" Killian said in disbelief. "Do you realize how much it changes things?"

"What do you mean?" Given the way they were acting, I guessed our being soulmates was a bigger deal than I'd thought. "We decided to be together."

"So you know about your connection and that it's unbreakable after you consummate it?" Griffin asked as he scrutinized my face for my reaction.

"Uh ... unbreakable?" I was supposed to be defusing the situation, but I had to know what that meant. "Sure. Aren't all soulmates unbreakable?"

"I tried to tell her before, but she kissed me." Alex hung his head, and his teeth retracted into his mouth. "And I lost my head."

Griffin shoved Alex in the chest and growled, "You're about to lose more than that."

This was still escalating. I needed to try another strategy. "Whatever *unbreakable* means, I'm okay with it." Though I'd be asking about all this later when Alex and I were alone. "I care about him and feel safe with him." And that meant so much to a girl like me. I'd never felt safe growing up, and even though Eliza and Annie were my rocks, I'd always felt something nudging inside me—a little bit of danger that both tempted me and scared the ever-loving shit out of me. That all disappeared when I was with Alex.

"Then why did you sound scared?" Sterlyn asked, her voice steady.

"This is going to sound crazy." I'd rather not share what I thought had happened, but my hands were tied. They'd know if I lied and think I was covering for Alex. "But ... I heard his voice in my head."

"You did?" Alex asked, sounding shocked. "What did I say?"

Ugh ... I hadn't thought this through. I didn't want to repeat what I'd heard, but there was no backing out. "I'm sure you didn't say this, but I heard, 'I love you.'" I stared at the floor, not wanting to see his denial.

"How is that possible?" Alex sounded confused. "You're human. I didn't expect you to be able to mind link."

I jerked my head up, focusing on him. "That's normal? And you did say, 'I love you'?"

"Well, I do love you," he said softly. "I didn't want to say it verbally because I didn't want to scare you off. A lot of stuff has been thrown at you."

I wasn't ready to say it back yet, but that didn't mean I didn't feel the same way about him.

An adoring smile filled his face. "No need to feel pressured to say it back."

No, he couldn't—"Did you *hear my thoughts*?"

He winked, back to his normal flirty behavior.

Him saying *I love you* didn't freak me out, but our

ability to communicate nonverbally did. Then, realization hit me. I pointed at Sterlyn and Griffin. "That's how you talk to each other! I thought you were communicating through expressions."

Sterlyn laughed. "Nope, not at all. Even though there are times he can tell I'm pissed without me saying the words."

"Yeah, her face grows cold, and she takes a deep breath." Griffin relaxed a little. He couldn't pass up the opportunity to tease her. "Breathing slow and deep always comes first."

"That is true." Sterlyn exhaled.

"Then how are you and Killian able to communicate nonverbally?" I had thought she was in a relationship with them both, but I'd learned she wasn't.

Alex chuckled like he'd heard my thoughts again.

This was going to be a problem. I glared at him. "Get out of my head."

Alex lifted his hands and beamed. "You're projecting your thoughts to me."

"I don't even know what that means." I blew a raspberry.

"Killian, Griffin, and I, along with several others, can talk telepathically because of our pack bond. Killian is the alpha of the guard pack here in Shadow Ridge, and Griffin is the alpha of both Shadow City and Shadow Ridge."

"*We* are the alphas of Shadow City and Shadow Ridge," Griffin corrected as he took his place by her side. "Sterlyn is also the alpha of the silver wolves."

Whoa, I was struggling to keep up. "Silver wolves? There are others like you?"

"Yes. My twin brother is leading them while Griffin and I get settled in Shadow City." Sterlyn yawned. "They live about twenty-five miles away. My uncle was their alpha, but he died a few weeks back, so we're figuring out the new leadership and how to work together."

That was understandable. Losing a family member was hard, and from my limited understanding, wolf hierarchy was important. "With you as their leader, I have a feeling everything will work out."

"I hope so," Sterlyn said and faced Alex. "You should've told her about the bond being unbreakable before linking your souls together. You said just kissing her in public put a target on her back. What do you think will happen now?"

"First off, I told her we were soulmates, and that having sex would change everything, but I couldn't give her specifics. I didn't know what our connection would be like because she's human." Alex took my hand. "And second, completing our bond will make it harder for them to attack. She's part of the royal family now. Harming her—hell, looking at her the wrong way would be a declaration of war. In a way, I *have* protected her."

"Man, you should know shit doesn't work like that." Griffin shook his head. "You saw everything Sterlyn and I went through. If anything, it'll make the rogue group more determined to use her as leverage."

"Not if she's with us all the time." Alex lifted his chin, appearing confident, even though I could feel a smidge of worry flowing through our connection. "After tonight, I can't leave her."

Maybe his arrogance was a ruse to make others fall in line more easily.

"Are you saying you want to stay here with us indefinitely?" Griffin frowned. "I thought this was a one-night thing."

"Until we can get Annie healed and figure out who is

behind everything." Alex placed an arm around my waist. "I'm thinking Klyn was part of the rogue group. Coming here was part obsession on his part but also retaliation, since we have Eilam locked up."

That made sense.

"So it was a power play." Sterlyn rolled her eyes. "If they're going to do crappy shit, why do they always have to hide? At least, own up to what you do and face the consequences head-on."

"At least, they know the face of their enemy," Griffin assured her as he kissed her cheek. "We didn't."

"Okay, it's time we all went back to bed." Sterlyn blinked like she couldn't keep her eyes open. "Since all seems well, finally, we all need our sleep. There's no telling what tomorrow will bring."

"Fine." Killian huffed and made his way to the door before turning back around. He cracked his knuckles and asked Alex, "Did you mess with her mind?"

"No. I could never do that to her." Alex patted his heart. "I swear to you, I will protect her and treat her right. I would give up my life for her."

The world stopped as I waited for Killian's reaction. I didn't think Alex had messed with my mind, but if he had, the truth would come out. But the intensity of my feelings for him had to be real.

Kilian bared his teeth. "Whether you like it or not, bloodsucker, Ronnie is part of our group, and we protect our own."

"Noted, and I'm glad you all care for her." Alex sounded sincere, and he tugged me closer. "You protected her while I tried to figure things out, and it took me about a week too long to realize that without her, I'd be miserable forever."

"And you say that Griffin and I are gag-worthy," Sterlyn teased. "Let's all get some sleep. I'm assuming I should bring your pillows and sheets in here?"

"Nah, I'll just sleep in bed with her." He kissed me and pulled back. "You're okay with that, right?"

The need to be close to him had grown stronger. There was no way in hell he was sleeping in the living room now. "Sure am."

"Well, all right." Killian tugged at his ear and averted his gaze. "If you guys do anything, and I do mean *anything*..." —his eyes widened to convey his meaning —"please, for the love of God, be quiet. I was half asleep and still heard some interesting noises from you two. I do not want to relive that, especially knowing you're newly mated."

I turned and buried my face in Alex's chest. I couldn't face Killian.

Alex wrapped his arms around me and chuckled. "No promises."

"Damn bloodsucker," Killian grumbled as he followed Sterlyn and Griffin out the door.

When the door shut, Alex swept me off my feet and carried me to bed. In his arms, I not only felt safe but light. He crawled into bed beside me and pulled me to his chest.

As my eyes grew heavy, I murmured, "I love you, too," and fell asleep without issue.

———

THE DOOR to our bedroom flung open, and my eyes fluttered. Reality filtered into my head as Sterlyn's floral, musky scent filled the room. She said, "You two need to get up. Someone is here to see you."

CHAPTER TWENTY-ONE

Alex's arms tensed around me, and I raised my head. Sterlyn stood at the foot of the bed. Her long silver hair was pulled into a ponytail, emphasizing the dark circles under her eyes. She was still gorgeous but looked a little worse for wear. I probably did too. Even in Alex's embrace, I hadn't gotten a restful sleep, listening for sounds of another attack.

Sunlight slanted through the blinds, informing me it was morning.

"Did something happen?"

She rubbed her arms. "No, but Alex needs to come out here before things escalate."

Something heavy formed in my chest.

"It's Matthew," Alex said and kissed my forehead. "He wants to *talk*."

"In other words, yell and threaten?" I hadn't missed his emphasis on the word, and I got that his brother was quick to anger.

Alex chuckled and placed a finger to his lips. "Got it?"

"Be quiet?" I got that he and I were a package deal, but that didn't mean he got to tell me to shut my trap. No one was allowed to do that but me. "That's rude."

"You didn't hear." He pointed to his head. "I projected something to you."

Oh, why wasn't it working? If it hadn't been for the warm connection in my chest, I would've been worried. As long as he wasn't telling me to be quiet, I wouldn't be upset. "No, there was nothing."

"Her human blood probably hinders the supernatural mind link at times," Sterlyn whispered. "But Alex, you need to get out there. He's vamped out."

"Yeah, that's not surprising." Alex stood and stretched, and his shirt rose above his pants. His toned abs peeked from underneath the hem, and my body warmed.

Alex didn't have a change of clothes. He'd need to go home and pack so he would be comfortable while staying here.

Then the importance of who our guest was sank in, and panic churned my stomach. "Wait, if Matthew is here, who's with Annie?"

"Gwen is there," Alex assured me. "I also asked her to keep an eye on Annie. She agreed, although I now owe her a favor."

If he trusted her, I should too. At least, she hadn't vamped out on me, so maybe it was better if she watched Annie anyway.

Sterlyn arched an eyebrow. "You guys use favors a lot, don't you?"

Alex shrugged. "It's the vampire way."

Begrudgingly, I scooted to the side of the bed and forced myself to get up. I could've stayed in bed all day, especially with Alex lying next to me, but Matthew had other plans.

"Stay here," Alex said then kissed me. "I don't want him taking out his frustrations on you."

"Fine." Normally, I'd be annoyed, but Matthew's vamped-out face still haunted me, and I wasn't too eager to see him again. "But I'm here if you need me."

"I know." He inhaled deeply and relaxed his face into its normal cocky expression. He looked at Sterlyn. "You're staying here with her, right?"

She nodded. "I'll stay."

He exhaled and strolled out of the room like he didn't have a care in the world, despite the dread wafting to me through our bond.

I couldn't let him face that alone. My legs propelled me to the door, but Sterlyn grasped my wrist. "It would be best if you stayed here. You did tell him you would."

She was right, but I'd agreed before I'd felt his trepidation. "Fine, but if they fight, the deal is off. I can't let him take the brunt of everything."

"None of this is your fault, but I understand." She snorted. "I'd be the same way. You're stronger together than apart."

Her words described how I felt perfectly. "Exactly."

"Matthew," Alex said from the living room. "I told you I wouldn't be coming back to the loft last night. Why are you here?"

"Oh, I got the text." Matthew's voice shook with anger. "And I responded, *Get your ass back here*, which you ignored."

"I wasn't asking for permission," Alex said in his cocky, unworried way. "You aren't my dad."

"But I am your king," Matthew growled. "And what I say is the law."

"Actually, what the council says is the law." Alex

snorted. "Unless there was a vote where the majority ruled that I had to return home, I'm fine. I doubt that happened since Sterlyn and Griffin never left the house last night, and I wasn't informed of an impromptu meeting."

"The council makes decisions for the city as a whole," Matthew countered. "*I* make decisions for the vampires, and you, Brother, fall under that umbrella."

Wow, his brother was an arrogant asshole. What kind of person wanted to dictate someone's every move?

Control freaks, that was who.

"You may be the king, but you're also my brother." Frustration laced through his laid-back tone. "And how did you figure out where I'm staying?"

"I have connections." Matthew laughed arrogantly.

"Or you were informed, like the rest of the council, when I called in the vampire death that occurred here?" Griffin interjected. "I told them Alex killed Klyn due to politics. I was going to let the council know this morning, but Matthew got here before I could."

Ugh, I hated that Griffin had made that call, but I understood he'd had to. There was resentment between the vampires and wolves.

"Yes, that's true, but I was already on my way here when I couldn't find Alex in his usual spots," Matthew said with disgust. "And you killed one of our own people who had already been detained? We could've gotten information from him."

"He tried to kill Veronica," Alex gritted out. "He had to die."

Even though I'd assumed Alex had killed Klyn last night, it was hard to hear him admit. He'd killed Klyn in cold blood, but I couldn't fault him. If someone tried to hurt him, I could very well do the same.

Matthew sounded annoyed as he said, "I guessed that the nuisance was here, which meant you'd be as well. It seems your streak of poor choices continues."

"She is not a nuisance," Alex growled. "Don't you dare talk about her that way."

I loved that he was standing up to his brother on my behalf, but I hated coming between them. As an orphan, I'd always longed to have a family, and Alex was damn lucky to have his. I wished we could be together without causing a rift between them.

"This has gone on far too long. I'm putting an end to this nonsense right now," Matthew bellowed. "Get outside. It's time you came back home."

Okay, that had escalated quickly. I hurried out the door with Sterlyn right behind me.

"Ronnie, wait." She grabbed my arm. "Are you sure you want to do this?" Concern reflected in her eyes.

"It's not fair for him to face this alone." Like she'd said minutes ago, we were stronger together. "I need to stand beside him." If I wanted to be part of this world, I had to push my fear aside; otherwise, the vampires would chew me up and spit me out.

Sterlyn blew out a breath. "Just stay beside one of us. It'll be safer that way. Okay?"

"Fine." I spun on my heel and headed toward the living room.

"I'm staying here," Alex said slowly, his voice level. "There's no way I'm leaving after Klyn's attack."

"Is this human girl worth it?" Matthew's voice dropped so low I could barely hear it. "Maybe I should eliminate the problem."

"If you try to kill her," Alex growled, "I don't care if you're my brother; I'll kill you myself."

"If you hurt Ronnie, you'll create problems with Alex and the wolves as well," Griffin said, stating the stakes clearly. "She's one of us."

"And more scrutiny will be placed on every vampire that crosses through Shadow Ridge," Killian added. "After all, you guys don't want us on your side of the river."

Sterlyn kept pace beside me, and the two of us entered the living room. Matthew stood against the wall, his hands fisted and his focus on his brother.

Surprisingly, Alex stood between Killian and Griffin. The three of them didn't get along, but they were presenting a united front and staring down Matthew.

Matthew's dark crimson eyes locked on me. His jaw dropped, and he hissed, "What the fuck? You *mated* with a human? I didn't even know that was possible. I knew you smelled different, but I never imagined *this*."

Okay, maybe coming out hadn't been the smartest move.

"I fought our connection, but I realized I didn't want to any longer. It may cause some unforeseen issues, but I refuse to do anything without Veronica by my side," Alex said sternly as he took my hand and pulled me behind him. "I refuse to live without her."

"You don't think I should get a say in who you mate with?" Matthew's laughter was devoid of humor. "You're the fucking prince. Everything you do reflects on me. We have a group of vampires rebelling against us, and you've helped ruin our reputation by having a human mate by your side."

My stomach lurched, but I kept my mouth shut. Alex had trusted us with that information, and Matthew would see him telling us as a betrayal.

"She's my soulmate." Alex wrapped an arm around me. "There's no going against the pull. She's the only one I want."

"You think she can give you heirs?" Matthew laughed hatefully. "She's human. A vampire child would tear her apart."

Alex's jaw clenched. "I don't care if I can't have children with her. She's the only thing that matters to me."

Wow. I'd never considered whether I wanted to have kids, but if being with Alex meant I could never bear children, I was more than okay with that, even if the thought stung.

"Heirs are part of our royal duty, especially since there aren't any yet." Matthew glared at me with so much hatred I nearly took a step back. "It doesn't matter. We will handle this problem later. She needs to stay here, and you need to come with me. We have things to take care of."

"I don't mind helping you, but I will come back here every night."

"Bring her with you to the loft." Matthew frowned. "There's no need to stay here."

Shadow Terrace was the last place I'd ever want to stay. Between the two attacks and Matthew glaring at me like he might kill me in my sleep, I didn't want to be anywhere near that town.

"She stays here," Alex said sternly. "And so do I. This is nonnegotiable."

"I bet they don't want you here." Matthew motioned to Griffin and Sterlyn. "So you should—"

"No, he's fine." Sterlyn smiled and laid her head on my shoulder. "Ronnie wants him here, which means he's welcome."

I wasn't sure how, but Matthew's face looked like an upside-down smile. That was how unhappy he was. I nearly felt bad for the guy.

Almost.

"Come on." Alex patted his brother's shoulder. "Let's get back and deal with the fallout of Klyn's death."

That snapped Matthew out of his funk. The older vampire's expression smoothed, and he nodded. "You're right. We need to get ahead of the story, and we can work out our strategy on the way there."

"There's nothing else to say, but okay," Alex said with frustration. He pulled me into his arms and kissed me until my toes curled.

The room faded away as his scent and taste consumed me. Our connection grew stronger as his love flowed into me. If I'd ever doubted his devotion, I never would again. We had fought our connection, and even though it had been only a short amount of time since we'd met, it felt like we'd known each other all our lives.

"Okay, now I see how people feel around us." Sterlyn laughed and nudged Griffin.

Killian sighed. "I would say I'm glad you finally figured it out, but now I have to watch two couples act like that all the time."

"Dude, you're just jealous." Griffin laughed. "One day you'll find your own girl. Hopefully, then you won't have to pretend to date someone."

"I don't understand what's going on here," Matthew grumbled. "Alex, we've got to go."

Alex pulled back and stared into my eyes as he whispered, "We'll continue this tonight."

My body warmed. "That better be a promise." I licked my bottom lip, tasting him.

"Oh, it's more than that." His flirty smile flitted across his face, and a deep need throbbed inside me.

"That's enough," Matthew groaned and jerked Alex's arm, pulling him away from me. "And I thought watching Gwen was horrible. At least she only sleeps with vampires and not our food."

"Watch how you talk about her," Alex snarled as Matthew opened the door and dragged his brother out. Before the door shut, he mouthed, *I'm sorry. I love you.*

The door slammed, and I stood there, feeling as if a piece of me had vanished. The sensation was so overwhelming I couldn't breathe. I clutched my chest as tears sprang to my eyes.

I hoped this day sped by because I wasn't sure I could hold out until he returned.

———

THE NEXT FEW days went by painfully slow. Every day, Alex left to help Matthew break Eilam and learn who might be part of his crew. Then, at sunset, Alex came back to Sterlyn and Griffin's house and joined our movie shenanigans.

For now, Alex and I had agreed to keep our relationship status secret from the vampire population. Not because we were embarrassed, but if our connection could cause more turmoil for the royal family and strengthen the rebel group's hold, we needed to hold out until we got Annie away from there.

I'd confided in him that Annie was not my biological sister but my adoptive sister and how we'd come to be a family with Eliza. And he'd told me stories about his parents. They'd been tough rulers, like

Matthew, but their love for each other had been inspiring.

I'd also learned more about our bond and how we could pull strength from each other and communicate telepathically. But our connection also made us vulnerable. When vampires lost their soulmates, they became closed off and hardened, more likely to succumb to their baser urges ... and lose their humanity. Without me and our soulmate connection to anchor him, Alex had been tempted when he'd attended Shadow Ridge University. A visiting human girl had been injured somehow, and because he hadn't been around humans, he'd nearly succumbed to his urges. That was one reason the university had visiting days so tightly set —so vampires could be monitored.

Also, vampire royalty wasn't much different from any other monarchy. As he'd told me previously, a human had made a deal with a demon, asking for power. The demon had toyed with the human, telling him all power came at a cost, and it had infused the human with demon-like abilities, the side effect being extreme bloodlust.

Because they were from that line, Matthew got to make the rules, and Alex and Gwen played the supporting siblings, doing his dirty work by working with their enemies to earn favors. If anyone guessed there was turmoil within the family, they might use it as leverage to push their own agenda.

Alex had said that when things settled down and I wasn't under constant threat, that I could attend the council meetings as an observer and hear the issues and trials the supernatural races in the city were struggling with. I wouldn't have an official voice in the matters, but he would always want to hear my thoughts and opinions. The idea of having a voice and improving people's lives stirred something inside me I'd never known I wanted. The chance to make a positive impact inspired me, exciting the restless part of me that I'd always battled with.

Though Rosemary, the wolves, and Alex had never said as much, they were getting used to one another. They still weren't best friends, but they weren't always at each other's throats either.

Tonight, Sierra had gotten her way with a modern remake of *Cinderella*. Alex and I placed blankets and pillows on the living room floor and got comfortable, Alex propped up on one elbow behind me, running his fingertips over my arm underneath our shared blanket. He didn't even pretend he was watching the movie.

"I'm hopeful," he whispered in my ear. "I think Eilam is about to break. It took much longer than I expected, but there's a chance that by tomorrow, Annie will be back to normal."

"Thank God." Each day, it felt like I would never get her back. Eliza was at the point of filing a missing person's report because I'd told her I hadn't seen Annie in over a week and some of my friends and I were working on it. I didn't know what else to do, and she was upset, thinking she'd done something wrong, and that Annie's situation was all her fault. I didn't have the heart to tell her that I wouldn't be coming home to Lexington when this was over.

One thing at a time. Once Annie was safe, we would plan how to integrate me into their world. The first step was introducing me to the council to see what we were up against with me being human. No matter what, Alex and I would be together, wherever that might be.

"I know it's been stressful, but the end is in sight," he said and kissed my shoulder.

"Stop." Sierra leaned over and pointed at us. "I get that

we're watching a romantic movie, but I don't want to see a reenactment on the living room floor. You lock that shit up."

"What did you expect when you insisted that you get the other end of the couch?" Killian glared at her. "At least, on the couch, they aren't in an easy position to do matey things. Look at Sterlyn and Griffin—they might kiss, but if they straddled each other, it would be obvious. His hands could be anywhere under there."

"Stop being prudes." Rosemary rolled her eyes. "Sex is fun and freeing. I don't know why you all get upset over it. If you don't like it, don't peek."

Of all the people to say that, I'd never dreamed it would be her.

I wasn't the only one who felt that way. Everyone but Alex stared at her. It was like I didn't know the person sitting there anymore.

Alex chuckled. "Who would've thought an angel and I would be on the same page?"

Oh my God. "We are *not* having sex in front of everyone."

"Ah, you're no fun." He winked at me. "But I have plenty of time to change your mind."

"I take it back." Sierra dry-heaved. "They're so much worse than Sterlyn and Griffin."

Alex's phone rang, and he groaned as he pulled it from his back pocket. *Matthew* flashed across the caller ID. "Figures." He answered it, ignoring Sierra's death glare. "Hello?"

Sterlyn tensed, able to hear what Matthew was saying on the other line.

Anxiety wafted from Alex. "I'm on my way." He sat up, his body rigid.

"What's going on?" Sometimes, I wished I had super-natural abilities. Okay, I often did.

"Eilam escaped." Alex stood. "Which means he'll be going after Annie."

CHAPTER TWENTY-TWO

I couldn't breathe. He was right. If Eilam had left, he would go straight to his coveted food source: my sister.

"We've got to protect her." I jumped to my feet and stepped toward the door.

A strong, familiar arm wrapped around my body. Alex rasped, "You have to stay put."

"Like hell I will." I got that I wasn't a supernatural badass, but she was my *sister*. I'd had a hard enough time sitting here this past week while he and Matthew had starved the creep, but my patience was at an end.

"Babe, you'll be a target." Alex's hold tightened. "As soon as they see us together, they'll know how damn important you are to me. If you want me to save Annie, I can't be worrying about you too."

"Who says they won't come here?" Being sidelined hurt. Didn't he understand I had to do this? "And what if I can help?" I'd be bait if that was what it took to save Annie.

"I love you, but *please*, let me handle this." He embraced me. "Eilam is focused on regrouping. Then he'll look for Annie or another human close by. He won't consider coming here for you at first, so it's safer for you here. What would happen if you got hurt? Annie would blame herself, and I would lose my damn mind."

Ugh, he was right. I was being stupid. What could I do over there? Bleed out and hope I got the right person to attack me? "Fine. But promise to be careful too. I can't lose —" A sob cut off my words. The idea of something happening to him was worse than anything I'd ever been through before. And that was just the thought. No way could I survive losing him.

"You won't lose me," he promised and brushed his lips against mine. "The vampire guards are already en route to the threat. It'll probably be over by the time I arrive."

He seemed awfully confident, but something was off. "If something doesn't feel right, get away."

"Will do." He released his hold on me and nodded at the others. "I'll be back soon."

"We'll keep an eye on her," Sterlyn said. "Don't worry about anything here."

"Thank you." He marched through the living room and out the door.

The front door shut, and panic rooted inside me as the yearning to go with him took hold.

"Hey, everything will be okay." Sierra sat on the floor and scooted over to me. "Alex is like a million years old. He knows what he's doing."

"That's older than Mom." Rosemary scoffed. "That's impossible."

Sierra glanced over her shoulder. "It's called sarcasm. I just meant he's old as dirt."

"I have to agree with Rosemary here." I tried to be in the

moment and tease, but my mind was preoccupied. "I don't like thinking of my boyfriend as old." Even if he was two hundred and eighty years older than me.

"First off, he'd be pissed if he heard you say *boyfriend*," Sierra said and pointed at Griffin. "Am I right?"

"Don't drag me into this." Griffin buried his face into Sterlyn's hair. "I'm just over here, minding my own business like you should be."

"Psh, yeah, right." Sierra waved him off and looked at me. "Second, whether you like it or not, he's pretty damn old." She lifted three fingers up. "And finally, I'm so tired of you siding with Rosemary. If you keep that shit up, I'll figure out ways to embarrass you, and I won't relent."

Yeah, she meant that. She was crazy but so damn loveable.

"You do realize you're a handful, right?" Killian arched an eyebrow and leaned back against the couch. "Even by supernatural standards."

"'Leave a lasting impression.'" She brushed her shoulders. "That's my motto."

Killian crossed his arms and shook his head. "You do that."

Even though they were trying to distract me, I couldn't stay still. "I'm sorry, but I'm going to head to my room for a few minutes."

"I'll go with you," Sierra said as she grabbed my arm, pulling herself to her feet.

I about tipped over but caught myself just in time. For her to be so thin, she was sturdy. "Whoa, how much do you weigh?"

"Hey, is that a fat joke?" She propped her hands on her hips and glared.

"No, I'm assuming it's a supernatural thing." Now I felt like an ass. I hadn't meant to imply there was anything wrong with her body type.

She patted my arm and laughed. "I'm just giving you a hard time, and yes, it's a supernatural thing. We're all strong and durable, so our size is misleading to humans."

That made sense. "As much as I appreciate you wanting to hang with me, I'd like to have a few minutes alone." Even though they felt like family, I was still a loner by nature. Being around people all the time wasn't the norm for me, and I needed time to get more acclimated.

"I'll be quiet as a mouse." She patted her chest, not letting it go.

Sterlyn snorted. "Let her have a second to herself. She's being nice, but she's newly mated, and he just left to walk into danger. She needs a moment to center herself."

Sterlyn's understanding made me feel a lot better. I didn't want to come off like an ungrateful brat, but I wasn't up to socializing right now.

Rosemary waved a hand at Sierra and said, "And we all know you can't be quiet."

Her bluntness had me smiling before I even realized it.

"Okay." Sierra bobbed her head from side to side. "You got me there. But if you aren't back out here in ten minutes, I'm coming in. There is no moping when I'm around. Got it?"

I didn't want to agree to her terms, but she wasn't giving me a choice. If I wanted even ten minutes of peace, I'd have to accept her terms. "Fine. Ten minutes."

"Go. Hurry," Killian said urgently, "before she changes her mind."

Taking his advice, I marched toward Alex's and my room. Just before I entered the hallway, Sierra smacked

Killian, making a huge whacking sound. She growled good-naturedly, "Don't reveal all my secrets."

"Do you actually have any secrets?" Killian snapped back, rubbing his arm.

Inside the bedroom, I shut the door and locked it. Not that it would do any good. There was still a key on the top of the doorframe.

I laid my head against the door and closed my eyes as emotions surged inside me. Annie was in danger, and so was Alex, even though he was determined not to admit it. I wasn't sure if he believed that was the case, or if he'd been saying it to reassure me. This was yet another time when being a supernatural would've come in handy. I'd have known if he'd given me a line of bullshit. I could ask Sterlyn and the others, but I didn't want to involve them more than they already were. Alex and the others were becoming friendly, and I didn't want to pit them against one another.

Unable to stand still, I paced the room, feeling something brimming under my skin. The only time I'd felt this sensation before was the night I'd arrived in Shadow Terrace. The feeling had attacked me before I'd reached the city entrance. Just like then, it had come out of the blue.

I scanned for the shadow, but nothing was here. Yet.

It had to be my nerves. I was stuck here, unable to help two of the people I loved most in the world. I was completely useless. All I could do was hope Alex and his family could protect Annie.

Ugh. I hated feeling like this.

I ran my hands through my hair and pulled at the tips until it hurt. I needed something ... anything to ground me from the horrible turmoil tearing me apart. I normally became on edge when Alex left, but this was more.

Like he was in danger.

My cell phone rang, and I jumped. I rushed to the end table and snatched up my phone, hoping it was Alex with an update. He had probably just gotten there, and maybe he'd been right and the fighting was over.

Without checking the caller ID, I swiped to answer and put the phone to my ear. "Is everyone okay?" Please God, let Annie be okay.

A dark chuckle filled my ear. "That depends on you. Are you alone?"

I pulled the phone away from my ear and glanced at the screen. The word *Restricted* scrolled across with no number.

That was what I got for not checking. I should've known better. "Yes, but how did you get this number?"

"Aw, are you scared, little one?" The deep voice sounded just like it had in the bar. "Did you forget that I have access to your friend's phone and contacts?"

Annie was so trusting she didn't even lock her phone. Not that it would have mattered. She'd have told him anything he'd asked.

I had to focus. The longer I remained silent, the more I'd thrill him. It hadn't taken me long to learn that about vampires. "No." I sounded breathless, contradicting what I'd said. I cleared my throat, needing to sound strong. "Why would I be scared of you?"

"Is that a serious question?" He laughed with delight. "I thought you figured out that I'm a vampire when you saw me drinking from your friend." He sighed in contentment. "Between the horror in your expression and seeing Matthew's vampire face, I was able to resist for that long in that piss-infested prison."

I was going to be sick. "Are you saying thinking of me made you hold out for that long?"

"Yes," he cooed. "And they say humans aren't smart."

"Why would that help you?" I didn't want to know, but if I was going to figure out his motive for calling, I needed the answer.

"Because I finally found something that matters to the royal family. You see, things are strained in Shadow Terrace, and we don't want to overthrow the royals. That would cause problems with Shadow City and put a target on our backs. But things need to change, and we finally have leverage against the monarchy to get them to meet our demands."

Alex was right. By claiming me, he'd made me of interest to others—and I wouldn't have it any other way. He was worth the risk. "What are your demands?"

"None of your concern." He sounded disgusted. "You're a human, and I don't need to discuss our agenda with you. But I do need you to meet me at the edge of Shadow Terrace."

"Why would I do that?" He must be insane if he thought I would willingly hand myself over to him.

"I'm so glad you asked." His voice grew animated. "I was able to grab someone very important to you and the prince. She's actually sitting here beside me."

No. If he'd just broken out of prison, how could he have done that? "You're bluffing."

"That's smart. It really is. But I can prove it." His foot-steps echoed on the line as if he were in a cave. "Annie, baby?"

"Yes," she responded breathlessly.

I'd never loathed anyone as much as I hated this man right now. He was ruthless, and I wondered if he could even walk in the sunlight. There was no way he could have any humanity left and be this way. I tried to find solace in the fact that Annie wasn't scared. Her being petrified would have made the situation much worse ... maybe.

"Do you mind getting on the phone and informing this person who is in this room with us?" Eilam asked.

"Of course," she said, and I heard movement as he handed her the phone. "Hello?"

"Annie." Tears sprang into my eyes, blurring my vision. "Are you okay?"

"I'm with Eilam, finally, so everything is better than okay," she breathed. "Gwen and her family tried to keep us apart, but I knew our love would win against all the odds, especially when I snuck some tainted blood into her drink."

Bile burned up my throat. I swallowed it down, trying to remain calm. "Is Gwen okay?"

"Not for much longer if I have anything to do with it." She snickered, and something like a kick sounded on the other end, followed by a groan of pain. "But Eilam says I get to punish her," she said happily.

Oh, dear God. He was going to make her torture Gwen. He was turning her into someone she wasn't. "Annie, you can't do that."

"But I can," she said defiantly. "I want to. She helped keep us apart."

If I hadn't seen her that day in the bar, I would've thought there was no way this was my sister and best friend. The goodness that radiated from her was no longer present. "Don't you remember—"

"Give me the phone," Eilam demanded, and I heard the same rustling in the background as she handed the phone back to him. "Meet me in the woods past the Shadow Terrace bridge. Someone will be there waiting for you. You have twenty minutes. You better come alone. If I see anyone else, I'll not only kill Annie but Alex's sister too."

"I thought you said you didn't want to hurt a royal." I hurried to the closet and slipped my tennis shoes on.

"Well, not the king or the spare." Eilam chuckled. "But the youngest one is fair game, especially when Alex will have you to blame for her death if you mess this up." He hung up, and the line went dead.

Even if I'd wanted to call him back, I couldn't. I didn't have his number.

Part of me wanted to sneak out the window and rush to Eilam, but that asshole couldn't be trusted. I couldn't be stupid. Without backup, neither Annie nor I would survive.

Even though I wasn't sure I was making the right decision, I swung open the door and headed into the living room.

All five of them looked at me as if they could tell something was wrong.

"Are Alex and Annie okay?" Sterlyn asked as she stood, ready to spring into action.

"No." Trying to hold my shit together, I informed them of my conversation with Eilam, but my panic leaked through. "I don't know what to do. He said to come alone, but that'll only get Gwen and me killed."

"You're right." Rosemary nodded. "I'll fly over and see if I can spot them."

"I have twenty minutes to get there." That meant I didn't have a minute to spare. That was probably why he'd given me that time limit. I had to act fast with no time to think.

"Go on and drive. I'll meet you outside the Ridge." Rosemary headed to the back door.

Sterlyn said, "We'll stop a few miles from the bridge so they can't see or hear us on the side of the road."

"Okay." Rosemary ran outside and took flight.

"Wait ... I knew you wouldn't stay behind, but he said for me to come alone. We *can't* show up together." There was no way in hell I could risk not only Annie's life but the life of Alex's sister too. What had I done?

CHAPTER TWENTY-THREE

I surveyed the room, looking for a way out of the house and to my car before they could catch me. Sterlyn riding with me was the very opposite of coming alone, and I couldn't risk Annie. But there was no way. Not with their super speed. Part of me regretted coming out here and informing them, but I wouldn't have gotten far either way. At least, this way, I'd retained their trust.

Sterlyn placed a hand on my shoulder. "We'll stay back far enough that he won't know we're there and wait until it's safe to strike."

Anxiety bubbled inside me, and I wrapped my arms around my stomach. This could go wrong in so many ways, and with each passing moment, that realization became clearer and clearer. "There's no way we're all getting out of this." Either Annie or I would die, and hell, there was a chance we both could. But I couldn't not try to save us all. I couldn't live with that.

"Yes, there is." Killian took my arm and tugged me toward him. He stared into my eyes, allowing me to feel the conviction of his words. "Sterlyn, Griffin, and I are trained for these types of situations. We won't let anyone die."

I glanced at the others. Their faces weren't wrinkled in disgust. Either they were purposely acting like they didn't smell a lie, or Killian believed what he said. I chose to bank on the latter for my sanity's sake. "Okay. Let's go. Time is running out."

"Should I be offended that you didn't include me in that pep talk?" Sierra grumbled as she headed to the garage. "I've been in my fair share of battles with you."

"You know I love you." Sterlyn followed her. "But there's a reason Killian left you out. You tend to freeze."

"That's because I didn't receive much training!" Sierra pouted and clutched the doorknob. "My family sent me to regular school instead."

Under normal circumstances, I'd find their banter funny, but it grated on my nerves. This wasn't a light-hearted situation, and the risk was real. Lives were at stake. Very important ones.

Not bothering to interrupt, I headed to the front door, ready to get into my car and go. They could either shape up or get left behind. Either way, I would save Annie and Gwen.

"Where do you think you're going?" Griffin asked, pausing in the foyer. "I know you need to take your car alone, but we all need to head out together."

"Eilam will be watching, so please don't follow too closely." And here they were, talking about how they'd been trained to think that way. "Otherwise, I might as well hold up a sign to kill Annie and Gwen right then and there."

"She's right." Sterlyn tapped her fingers against her leg. "We don't need to take our vehicle anyway. It'll only draw attention. Why don't you three shift, and I'll ride with

Ronnie until we pull over before the bridge and wait for Rosemary's update."

Despite hanging out with them all this time, I'd never seen them in their animal form. Some discomfort eased through me despite my curiosity, but they would blend in better that way.

"Fine," Griffin growled and kissed her.

I opened the door, and a cool breeze brushed against my face, invigorating me. I hadn't noticed how worked up I was until that moment. I inhaled, letting the cool air fill my lungs.

A man dressed all in black that I'd never seen before stood at the corner of the house, looking for something ... a threat. This had to be a guard. A thought that should have calmed me but didn't.

I pulled the keys from my pocket, and my hands shook so much that I almost dropped them. I clutched them and pressed the unlock button. Sterlyn breezed past me and climbed into the backseat then hunkered down.

I'd never been as envious of someone as I was her. Even in the face of adversity, she had an air of confidence, while I was a shaking mess. If I could have just an ounce of her composure, I would be way better off.

Trying not to overanalyze it, I opened the driver's door and slid into my seat. I started the car and took a second to calm myself. "Do you think they have someone watching us?" I didn't want Eilam to know I wasn't coming alone so soon.

"No. We have both Shadow City and Shadow Ridge guards keeping watch around the property," Sterlyn said. "And I don't see anything out of the ordinary. They'd have a *very* hard time getting here undetected after that guy's attack."

Klyn.

The prick who'd gotten what he deserved.

I put the car in reverse and pulled onto the street. As we drove away from the house, a honey-blond wolf charged toward us and ran next to the car, its thick fur reflecting the light. Its tongue partially hung from its mouth as its muscles contracted.

My hands tightened on the steering wheel as if anticipating the wolf to run in front of our car. If I hadn't already been a nervous wreck, that would have put me over the edge. "Can you please tell whoever that is to cool their jets?"

"His jets?" Sterlyn chuckled and shifted behind me. "And yes. Griffin's just a little intense at times."

"Rosemary is intense." I'd never seen anyone as serious as her, but it was hard to describe her. She was reserved but outspoken, which normally didn't go hand in hand, but it worked for her. "He's more like *growlfully* aware."

As if he'd heard me, Griffin growled so loud and deep that I could hear him from inside the car. He took off toward the woods that backed up onto the neighborhood, then I saw wolves who had to be Sierra and Killian running by.

"Yeah, I can see that." She hunkered back down onto the floorboard. "It'll take us about ten minutes to get to the spot where Rosemary will be."

I accelerated and followed the road out of the neighborhood and toward the town's exit. Part of me screamed to go back, that I didn't know what I was getting myself into. But that was my fear talking. I gripped the steering wheel, hoping it would ground me. "How do you keep calm in stressful situations?" Maybe if she gave me some tips, I could handle this a little better.

"When we said we were trained for this, that wasn't an exaggeration." Sterlyn exhaled. "Those of my race were the original guards of Shadow City. We left because we were persecuted by Azbogah after he learned we're part angel, but we continued to train for the time we would resume our original purpose—protecting the entire supernatural species. We're called the protectors, and within the first five years of our lives, we begin our training."

"Five?" That was so young. I must have misheard.

I glanced in the rearview mirror.

"Yeah. Nothing strenuous at first. More endurance training, like running in both human and wolf form."

"That's the worst kind of training." I remembered gym class and having to run laps and play dodgeball or whatever sport of hell they'd decided on that day. "I'd rather lift weights any day."

She laughed. "Yeah. Maybe. But my point is, to reach the endurance level we need, we learned controlled breathing."

"Okay?" I tried not to sound confused, but my voice had gone up about ten octaves.

"How about this?" She touched my arm. "When you get nervous or scared, what are some of your physical responses?"

That was easy. I was experiencing them now. "Racing heart, sweaty palms, rapid breathing, and dizziness."

"Exactly. Each one is a reaction to not getting enough air. If you control your breathing, the other things won't affect you as much. Try it."

What was the worst thing that could happen? Might as well give it a go. I slowly filled my lungs then exhaled. After doing it a handful of times, my mind wasn't nearly as fuzzy. "You're right."

"See?" she said. "Remember that, because you're about to enter a situation where your body will try to control you. You have to remember to keep calm and breathe because you'll have to think clearly and objectively. Griffin, Sierra, Killian, Rosemary, and I will do everything we can to keep you safe. But I won't lie. Some of that will depend on you, and if you can't control your body, you won't be able to think clearly."

She was right. No matter how much they promised that nothing would happen, it wasn't like any of us had a crystal ball. If we did, then we wouldn't be in this situation. "Any other tips or tricks you can bestow?"

"Yeah." I heard shuffling behind me; then Sterlyn's arm popped between the seats, holding something out to me. "This is my security blanket, and I want you to borrow it for the night."

She was holding a dagger in her hand. The handle was dark silver with a full moon etched in the metal. "I ... I can't take that. It obviously means something to you."

"It does, but your life is more important. Besides, I can't use it in wolf form." Sterlyn placed the dagger on the center console. "You're like family to me, and I need you to be able to protect yourself. They'd find a gun easier than this. It'll fit under your jeans around your ankle. Luckily, you like to wear bootcut like me. Don't pull it out unless you absolutely need it."

"Okay." She'd loaned me her knife, and it meant so much. Not only that but having a way to defend myself made the situation feel not quite so hopeless. "Thank you."

She patted my shoulder. "I'm just allowing you to borrow it. I expect it back once you and Annie are safe."

"You really do know what you're doing." I laughed, surprising myself. I'd felt so scared and unprepared—and hell, I still did—but Sterlyn made me feel like I was a worthy adversary. She was giving me the tools to survive. She'd done basically as much for me in this short time as Eliza and Annie had for me, which warmed me toward her even more.

The intersection that led to Shadow Terrace or back toward human civilization loomed in front of me. If I turned left, I was heading toward the vampire and chaos. Just a few weeks ago, I'd had no clue what I was driving into. Even though I wished Annie's life had never been at risk, I couldn't regret coming here.

By having my entire life stripped bare, I'd found the love of my life, the one person fate had designed solely for me, and a family I'd never known I was missing.

In other words, I'd found myself, and despite not being supernatural, this was where I was always meant to be.

I drove left as darkness surrounded us, drawing us deeper into the night toward creatures that had lost so much of their humanity they couldn't even bear the moonlight, unless they were covered from head to toe.

"Pull over here." Sterlyn's head popped up beside me, and she pointed to a gravel section off the road just wide enough for my car. "Griffin, Sierra, and Killian are almost here."

"Do you think we're enough?" I knew we couldn't risk bringing more of their people. Shifters weren't allowed in vampire territory, and the more people we brought, even in wolf form, the more detectable we'd be.

I buckled the knife in its sheath around my right ankle like Sterlyn wore it, and having it there made me feel a little safer.

"Yes, the vampire won't expect us to jeopardize relations by going onto their land." She leaned forward, examining the sky and then our surroundings. "He'll expect Alex to do something, not us. So the smaller numbers will work in our favor." She opened her door. "Come on. We're alone, and Griffin just informed me that they're close by, and Rosemary is landing."

Listening, I got out of the car and moved to stand beside her. The sky was dark, and now that my headlights were off, I couldn't see much of anything. Sterlyn's skin glowed in the moonlight, and that was the only thing keeping me from losing my head.

Paws padded toward us, and I assumed it was Griffin and the others since Sterlyn didn't seem alarmed.

I heard wings, and Rosemary soon landed in front of us. Three sets of glowing eyes appeared across the road, and the wolves ran toward us.

Rosemary didn't wait for them to reach us. "Two vampires are standing in the middle of the road a few feet past the bridge, waiting for her. Nothing else. Something doesn't feel right."

"Are they covered from head to toe?" The images of the vampires walking the streets in the darkness decked out in clothes flickered in my mind.

"No, they're dressed normally, which doesn't make sense." Rosemary scratched her head. "Maybe she shouldn't go."

"I've got to." They had to understand. "He has our sisters."

As my eyes adjusted to the darkness, the dirty-blonde wolf trotted up beside me and nodded. Even in wolf form, Sierra had my back. Maybe I shouldn't have been so hard on her earlier.

"Fine." Rosemary groaned. "I'll take to the sky and stay as low as possible without being detected. Two of you should stay on one side of the road and two on the other. You won't be able to walk across the bridge—you'll have to swim across the river from one wooded area to the other."

Sterlyn nodded. "Okay."

"Is that safe?" I didn't want to risk one group of friends for another. I loved these guys as much as Annie.

"We're wolves." Sterlyn gave me a thumbs-up. "We're good swimmers. I promise."

"Let's get this over with." Rosemary flared her wings. "And don't do anything stupid." She took off again.

I stood there in awe, watching Rosemary fly higher and higher into the sky.

"Go ahead and get in the car." Sterlyn pointed to the woods. "I'm going to go shift. When you see me come out, give us a two-minute head start before going over the bridge."

The clock mocked me. "Okay, but hurry. I need to be there in three minutes."

Sterlyn sprinted into the woods, and my heart raced as sweat dripped down my neck. My head grew dizzy as I stumbled to the car and got back in.

Dammit. I had to breathe. I wasn't even in danger yet, and I was already forgetting to keep my head clear.

I'd inhaled and exhaled five times before Sterlyn came barreling from the tree line. She was even more gorgeous in wolf form than in human form, and she was huge, her silver fur shining in the moonlight.

Griffin ran toward her, and they took off to the right, while Killian and Sierra went left. I watched the clock, waiting for two minutes to go by.

Time seemed to stand still.

After what felt like hours, my two minutes were up, and I pulled back onto the road. The trees thickened as the bridge appeared up ahead. I crossed the bridge, and just as Rosemary had said, two vampires stood there, waiting for me, about a hundred yards away. One looked harsh and cold, and the other seemed young because his face had never lost its baby fat.

The one with hardened features lifted a hand, signaling for me to stop, and a sinister smile spread across his face.

My head screamed *no*, but there was no turning back now.

CHAPTER TWENTY-FOUR

I slowed the car in the center of the road. There was hardly any traffic here, and if someone did come across my car, part of me hoped they would stop to see what was wrong.

For Eilam to have called me and sent men here to meet me meant Alex had grossly underestimated the man's pull. Somehow, Eilam had escaped and hidden away in this city, which seemed crazy. The town wasn't sizable by any means.

The man who had signaled me to stop glided toward me, the shadows of his sharp cheekbones adding a deadly glint to his crimson eyes. He opened my door, his body tensing under his black shirt. "Get out." His tone was soft but threatening.

Panic clawed inside me, taking over my body.

"Why don't you give her a second, Darick?" the round-faced vampire said, sounding concerned. With that baby face, he didn't appear any older than me. His short, styled honey-blond hair stood out in the moonlight, and his skin looked practically alabaster, especially against his black clothing. "Can't you hear how fast her heart is racing? We don't want her to have a heart attack." His voice dropped. "Before we've fed from her."

And here I'd hoped he might be less inclined to hurt me.

Darick inhaled. "You'll be the reason she doesn't last that long, Zaro. Don't play head games with her. It's not time."

Breathe, Ronnie, I chastised myself. Sterlyn had given me the key to keeping my cool, and at the first chance to use her advice, I was blowing it. I inhaled deeply, forcing my lungs to fill completely. I had to override my body's instincts, which was harder than I'd expected. My lungs didn't want to work, so it was like the air chipped away at my insides. The amount of discomfort it took to breathe was surprising, but it eased some of my panic.

A shiver ran down my spine. We were being watched. I hoped the sensation came from Sterlyn and the others and not more vampires.

Shit. The shifters were on this side of the river. I hadn't considered the consequences until this moment. Hopefully, if it became a problem, Alex could fix it.

What's ... Alex's voice popped into my head, and I almost screamed. *Veronica.*

What's Veronica? What the hell kind of question was that?

Our connection felt like it had bad reception, reminding me of the old walkie-talkies I used to have with a neighbor. At least, Alex and I were able to connect a little.

Wrong? His voice broke through again. *Hurt?*

"Move," Darick said, pulling me back to the moment. "Each second you make him wait puts your friends at greater risk. Unless you don't care if they make it out alive."

"I don't know where to go," I lashed out. My conflicting

emotions and uncertainty had me so scared that I was getting angry. "So why don't you freaking lead the way?"

"Oh, she's feisty." Zaro waggled his eyebrows. "That makes it more fun to break them."

It didn't matter what I did. Any reaction confirmed that I was their prey. The best thing I could do was not react until they forced my hand.

I turned off the car, concentrating on keeping my hands as steady as possible. Even with my complete concentration, they still trembled. I removed the keys, placing them in my pocket as I stood. I wanted to fight these two here and now, but that would only piss off Eilan and guarantee that Annie and Gwen would be hurt. I had no clue where they were hiding.

"Good girl," Darick cooed as he grabbed my arm. His cool fingers dug into my skin. Even through my shirt, the coldness seeped into my bones.

He dragged me toward the tree line, and I scanned the area for any sign of the wolves. Silver lavender eyes peeked briefly through some branches before disappearing again.

I'd only ever seen one pair of eyes that color. Sterlyn was letting me know she was here.

Feeling marginally better, I focused in front of me and tried not to let on that others were close by.

"Don't try to escape." Darick pulled me against his chest, and his cotton candy scent caused saliva to pool in my mouth. "We're faster than you, and all you'll wind up doing is allow Zaro to have immense fun tormenting you."

Yeah, Zaro put on the nice-guy act until the malice peeked through, making him unpredictable. With Darick, I knew what I was getting. His features matched his sullen demeanor.

We walked into the thickening maple, sycamore, and

oak trees. Alarm shot through me. I'd expected them to get in the car with me or have a car waiting. "Where are you taking me?"

"It's a surprise." Darick *tsk*ed as he cut his eyes at me. "Do you think we'd be foolish enough to tell you?"

His words rubbed me the wrong way. He had no reason to gloat and no reason not to tell me. I wanted to ask more questions, but they'd just gloat more, so I kept my mouth closed and forced my body to relax—a damn impossible task.

About a quarter of a mile into the woods, Zaro stopped in front of an area with wild ginseng brush.

I glanced over my shoulder, taking in my surroundings. We were in the middle of nowhere. Eilam had to be around, but I couldn't see a trace of anyone.

The corners of Darick's mouth tipped upward. "What's wrong? Something not sitting right with you?"

A siren rang in my head. They had something planned, something we hadn't expected.

Zaro squatted down and lifted a clump of ginseng from the ground. My eyes widened as he revealed an opening the size of a manhole.

A strong arm wrapped around my waist, and Darrick carried me to the hole, making the world blur around me. He jumped in, and my stomach lurched as we dropped into an endless abyss. The cold, damp air rushed past my body, and a scream strangled my throat. No amount of deep breathing would regulate this kind of trauma.

I closed my eyes, bracing for impact. It had to come soon. The image of Alex popped into my head, and I held on to it. *I love you.*

Veronica. His panic intertwined with mine, and I felt

even more out of control. *Where the hell are you?* Our connection was crystal clear.

My body jarred as Darick's feet hit the ground, and I exhaled shakily and opened my eyes. Darkness surrounded me. *I ... I don't know. Down a hole in the woods.*

Something overhead slammed shut, and footsteps sounded. Zaro was climbing down what had to be a ladder. It couldn't be stairs since we'd dropped straight down.

Darick cradled me in his arms and took off running. The cool air hurt to breathe, and the chill of his body and the tunnel's temperature made me ache with shivers. With all four my friends in wolf form, they wouldn't be able to open the hatch, but Rosemary could. It was as if the vampires had anticipated that the wolves would follow me.

Please tell me you didn't come here. Alex's voice broke inside my head, and fear radiated off him. *Eilam can't be found.*

I ... I'm underground somewhere on the Shadow Terrace side with two vampires named Darick and Zaro. I winced, dreading his reaction. *Eilam called me. He has Annie and Gwen.*

The bastard. But what part of staying put did you not understand? I can't handle you being in danger, Alex hissed. *How did you get away from Sterlyn and the others?*

They came with me. We split up before I crossed the bridge so no one would see them following me. Maybe this hadn't been the brightest idea, but what else was I supposed to do? Eilam had two people who meant so much to Alex and me. *I thought we were being smart, but the vampires brought me into an underground tunnel.*

Silence was the response for so long I figured our connection had cut out again. A light flickered in the distance, and I blinked to make sure I wasn't seeing things.

Within seconds, the dim light surrounded me, allowing me to take note of my location.

The inside was all concrete with mold growing on the walls. A bulky barred gate ahead of us swung open.

"Hurry!" Zaro said urgently behind us. "I hear wings—an angel is coming."

"An *angel?*" Darick hissed. "Why is a fucking angel involved?" He picked up the pace, and I grew dizzy.

"Shut up and run," Zaro snapped.

As soon as he'd run through the door, he stopped and dropped me on my feet then turned. Once Zaro had sped through, Darick slammed the door shut and locked it, sliding the key inside his pocket.

I had to get that door open so Rosemary could get in. I squatted and pulled the dagger from the sheath then kept it cradled at my side.

"Come on." Darick snagged my arm and dragged me away just as black wings became visible.

There she was. If only I could get her the keys. Not wanting to overthink my next actions, or else I'd freeze, I clutched the dagger and swung it at the vampire, aiming for his heart. I hoped and prayed it didn't take a wooden stake to kill them, or I was screwed.

I hit the mark. The dagger sliced through Darick's chest like butter until the handle hit the skin. Eyes widening, he stumbled backward and grabbed his nose. Blood poured from his chest and soaked his shirt.

"What the—" Zaro's gaze landed on me, and hate filled his eyes. "Aren't you stupid?"

Yeah, I probably was. I reached into Darick's pocket right when Rosemary reached the gate. Her dark purple eyes shone as she grabbed the gate and tried to yank it off the hinges.

My hands felt the cool metal of the key, and I pulled it out. Zaro grabbed me and threw me over his shoulder, hitting my stomach hard. I gasped through the pain. He leaned down and removed the dagger from Darick's chest and chuckled. "Thanks for the gift."

"You bastard. Let me in, and I'll kill you mercifully," Rosemary demanded as she gritted her teeth, straining to get through the doors.

A howl echoed inside the tunnel. Sterlyn and the others had made it down the hole.

"I'm not worried." He faced the opposite direction, ready to take me deeper into the tunnel. "That's angel-proof metal, so no supernatural can get through it. No amount of pulling will work."

Hoping he wouldn't notice, I pretended to cough and lifted my hand to cover my mouth, getting ready to toss the key to Rosemary. But as I went to lob the key, Zaro spun around causing me to drop it.

"Not so fast." He laughed and bent, snatching the key from the ground. "Did you really think I wouldn't see through your charade?"

The wolves came into view, running toward me.

But my hope was lost. If Rosemary couldn't get through the bars, I assumed they couldn't either.

Maybe if I bought them time, they could figure out a way inside.

Zaro stood and stepped deeper into the tunnel when I blurted out, "Are you just going to leave Darick there?" I focused on the man, who appeared to be dead.

Well—officially dead.

His chest didn't move.

"He underestimated you. I have more pressing matters to deal with than disposing of his body." He increased his speed, and I glimpsed at my friends longingly one last time.

Sterlyn growled deep, and Rosemary continued to tug on the door. Killian and Griffin were looking for another way in while Sierra watched me with sad eyes, whimpering.

I closed my eyes, not wanting this to be the last way I saw my friends.

I thought of Alex again and pretended I could speak with him, trying not to fall apart. That would be too easy for them. *Rosemary and the others can't get through this gate in the tunnel. The vampires locked them out.*

It doesn't matter, Alex responded. *I'll find a way through. I'm following the pull of our bond. Whatever you do, stay alive until I get there.* His voice broke. *I don't know how he did it, but it's like he vanished into thin air.*

The tunnels lead somewhere. I can't tell how far we've run because the vampires move too fast, but Rosemary, Sterlyn, and the others are down here too. The entryway is under some wild ginseng bushes, about a quarter mile into the woods south of the bridge.

Just stay strong and keep him talking. Alex didn't sound like the cocky man I'd fallen for. *Eilam loves hearing himself talk.*

Most egotistical men did.

The blood rushed to my head as Zaro lazily strolled ahead. My hair hung down into my face, and with each step, his shoulder dug into my side.

A door creaked open, and I lifted myself enough to see a wooden door like you'd find in any house. When he stepped through it, the air didn't warm. If anything, it felt chillier.

"I was beginning to wonder if you would ever get here." Eilam's nasal voice grated on my nerves.

"We ran into some problems," Zaro said with disgust as he placed me on my feet.

The basement was all concrete like the tunnel, but the walls and floor were clean. A maroon rug lay in the middle of the room with a loveseat on the edge.

I gasped.

Annie was straddling Eilam with her head tilted to the side. Blood trickled down her neck from two puncture holes near the collar of her violet shirt, staining it, and dripped from the corners of his mouth as his dark, soulless eyes latched onto me. He licked away the excess blood and groped her in front of me. "Where's Darick?"

"She killed him. And an angel and four wolves are in the tunnel looking for her."

His eyes flashed with anger. "I told you to come alone. Now you've forced my hand." He grabbed Annie's ass and lifted her off him. She whined and tried to crawl back on. "One second, my pet. I'm not done with you."

As he stood, his eyes focused on one corner of the room.

I followed his gaze, and my stomach dropped.

CHAPTER TWENTY-FIVE

G wen was chained in the darkest corner of the room. Her ivory, blood-streaked hair hung in her face, and the dark circles under her eyes were the same shade as her chestnut irises. She wore dark denim jeans that were ripped at the knees, and from the scabs peeking through, I was pretty sure they hadn't been designed that way. She had her arms wrapped around her bare belly, right under the hem of a dingy white crop top.

"What did you do to her?" None of this made sense. Why would he piss off the royal family?

"I'm returning the favor to your brothers for what they did to me," Eilam explained and sauntered over to Gwen. He ran his fingers through her hair as if she were an animal. "I'm bleeding her out, so she'll need to feed more. Then I'll unleash her and let her kill you and Annie. She'll lose some of her humanity, making it easier for her to succumb to the next few kills, until she loses it all."

In other words, become more like him.

This asshole was truly heartless.

"I'll never turn into someone like you." She sneered,

and her eyes flicked to me. "Even an underground compartment in the blood bank can't stay hidden forever."

I needed to tell Alex, and our connection strengthened when I was highly emotional. Strong emotions enhanced it somehow.

Ugh. Now that I wanted to panic, I couldn't. *Alex!* I tried, but silence answered me.

Eilam lifted his hand and stared at a hulking ring on his finger. "You have to admit, it is poetic. The very building we use to retain our humanity has helped so many lose it."

His ring reminded me of a high school class ring or a family crest like people had worn several centuries ago. He adjusted it so it was perfectly centered on his ring finger and punched Gwen in the jaw.

The intricate design of crossing swords marked her face, and blood trickled down from the bottom of the design.

"Stop! Don't hurt her." The panic I desperately needed filled me. *Alex, we're in a hidden underground room in the blood bank.*

What? I'm with the wolves, and that's why Sterlyn can smell so much blood. Rage laced each word. *We're already halfway back to town. The wolves are trying to sniff out where you are, so we'll be there in minutes. Whatever it takes, keep him talking.*

Yeah, that was easier said than done. *I'll try. He has your sister chained up, and he's beating her. His plan is to release her and let her attack Annie and me.*

It won't come to that. He paused. *But she'll need to heal, and the best way to do that is by feeding. If he lets her go, do whatever you have to in order to protect yourself. Even if it means—*He cut off as pain wafted between us. His voice broke as he said, *Even if it means hurting her. Just don't let her become like him. She wouldn't want that.*

Great. No pressure. But I was part of this world now. Not only did I have to learn to live in it. I had to embrace it.

A shadow flickered across the room, drawing my attention. My eyes widened, and my heart stuttered. I couldn't make out its face, but the shadow was crawling toward me—just like when I was a kid. That damn thing showed up every time I was in a horrible situation as if it fed off my turmoil. This made the situation even more terrifying.

Focus, Ronnie. It's your imagination. If I didn't get my shit together, Eilam would get what he wanted. "Why are you hurting people when you have an entire blood bank at hand?" They probably coerced human visitors into giving blood. Why hurt humans and some of their own?

"Do you know how much sweeter blood tastes and how much stronger it makes us when we drink straight from the tap?" Eilam's eyes flicked to Annie. "Drinking donated blood is like taking a drug substitute to get by instead of having the real thing."

Maybe that was why killing was easier after their first taste. It was an addiction. "But you haven't killed Annie." I winced as soon as the words had left my mouth, wishing I could take them back. It sounded as if I was goading him to do it.

"Her blood is different. There's something to it I've never tasted before. A slight bitterness, mostly hidden, and it intrigues me. I'm not willing to give her up yet." Eilam turned to ogle my friend. "That's the only reason she's still around."

Annie giggled. "I love you too, baby."

Oh, dear God. Gag me. "I still don't understand." I tried bringing him back to the question at hand. "Why have this room underneath a blood bank?"

Eilam licked his lips. "Each day for the past decade, I

worked here, draining human blood. Do you know how hard it is to smell the warm blood going into the bags? Why should we deny who we are? We were made this way. So, a handful of us decided to drink straight from the humans. Of course, we have to keep the blood banks operational for those vampires too scared to drink from the source—the threat of retribution from the royals and the other races who don't understand keeps them in line. But it's time for a great awakening, and for whatever reason, the young prince is obsessed with *you*, so the timing is perfect. If his sister kills you, it'll eat at his soul and allow his true nature to take over."

My throat closed as terror coursed through me. He didn't want to use me as leverage. He wanted to force Alex to lose his humanity to get over the heartbreak of my death. Was that possible? I didn't want to know.

"You'll never turn the royal family into one of you." Gwen lifted her chin. "We won't succumb to our desires like you have. We're stronger than you."

"Oh, you will." Eilam rubbed his hands together. "This will make you see things for what they really are." He removed a key from his pocket and approached the chains.

"You can't even go out during the day. How the hell does that make you stronger?" I'd moved to jump him when Zaro's arm wrapped around my body.

He *tsk*ed. "Nuh-huh. No misbehaving."

"Not having a nagging conscience is how." Eilam glanced over his shoulder. "Being able to do what you want without guilt or remorse is freeing."

He didn't get that losing his humanity actually took away his freedom, tying him to the night and allowing his desires to overwhelm him. "How is that freeing? It sounds like you've imprisoned yourself."

"Did you hear that?" Zaro said loudly, his body stiffening against me. "Someone is here."

I'd heard nothing, but that wasn't surprising with my human ears.

Eilam tensed and glanced around the room. "Impossible! How in the hell could they find us?"

Footsteps pounded above us, and someone yelled, "They're somewhere near here. Search high and low. There must be a secret passage."

Eilam's nostrils flared, and he clutched the key. "Someone must have betrayed us."

"It doesn't matter." Zaro shoved me to the floor. "Just let the princess go, and let's get this over with."

My stomach sank, and I forced air into my lungs as the shadow inched closer. *Get your ass here quick,* I connected to Alex. *Things are hitting the fan.*

We're here, Alex snarled. *We ran into an issue with Matthew because Sterlyn and the others are here.*

A howl echoed in my ears, the wolves confirming their presence. Hope blossomed, warm inside my chest. Together, the group was capable of anything.

"They brought fucking wolves," Eilam muttered and unlocked Gwen's chains. "How the hell did that happen? They're not allowed in Shadow Terrace even if they are friends with her."

"I don't know," Zaro said.

With the pressure of the chains gone, Gwen sank to the ground. A small whimper escaped me as I took in the brutal way they'd treated her. My hands clenched into fists.

Her wrists were bloody from spikes set inside the cuffs. When Eilam had said he was hurting Gwen, he'd meant it beyond what I could see with my own eyes.

Eilam kicked her in the stomach, and she curled into a ball. He growled, "Go feed. Now."

"No!" she yelled, her body shaking with pain and hunger. "I refuse."

The footsteps grew louder, but they didn't sound close enough.

"You will," Eilam hissed. He grabbed her wrist and stuck his finger inside a cut, making the injury bleed even more. "Zaro, cut her." He jerked his head my way. "Make her bleed."

"I'd be more than happy to." Zaro fisted my hair, pulling me from the floor and into his chest. He brought Sterlyn's dagger to my neck. "This is sweet justice, wouldn't you say?"

The dagger bit into my neck, burning as my blood spilled. Tears filled my eyes, but I pushed them back.

Veronica, hold on, Alex connected.

What did he think I was doing! I channeled my annoyance so I could focus.

"No!" Gwen whimpered. "Stop." Clapping her hands over her mouth and nose to mask the scent, she rocked back and forth.

"Bring her over here." Eilam kicked Gwen in the face.

Her nose cracked with a sickening crunch that I heard, even with my non-supernatural ears, and blood flowed between her fingers.

It's getting bad. I wasn't sure whether Alex could hear me, but I had to try something. "Leave her alone!"

Zaro lowered the knife and jerked me by the head. My neck cracked, and a stabbing pain shot down my spine and through my limbs until my body felt like it was on fire. My stomach rolled.

My legs crumpled beneath me, and I spasmed, losing

control over my body. As Zaro dragged me toward Gwen, bringing the temptation within her reach. I tried pushing against the ground to stop our forward motion.

"Stop!" I cried, desperation flooding me. I wasn't getting out of this.

Alex connected with me, his desperation mixing with mine. *We're searching for a way in.*

I love you. I needed him to know.

"We've got to find them now!" Alex shouted from above.

Zaro hovered over me, and I could feel Gwen's cool body next to mine.

A sob racked her body, and the stark realization that I wouldn't make it out of here alive slammed through me. I wasn't sure how long she could resist in her current state.

"Feed from her," Eilam pushed Gwen's head in my direction. "Now."

"No!" she cried. "Never! I'd rather die."

"You say that now, but you don't mean it." He sniggered. "That's what they all say at first."

Holy shit. He'd been *forcing* vampires to feed this way? What kind of sicko was he?

"Cut her again," Eilam said. "Make it deep."

I had to do something. Playing the victim was no longer an option. At this rate, I was going to die, either from Zaro or from Gwen.

The footsteps above were getting closer, but it sounded like they were still hunting for the door. They were close, but not close enough to save me.

Not sure what else to do, I turned to the shadow, my back now facing Gwen. The shadow stopped and turned its head in confusion.

"Please kill him," I asked it. I felt stupid, but I was desperate.

"Who are you talking to?" Zaro glanced in the direction of the shadow.

Eilam said with disgust, "She must have injured her head. Ignore her."

"Fine." Zaro grabbed my shoulder, forcing me onto my back, and lifted the dagger above my chest, holding it with both hands as he straddled me. "If she has a fatal wound, there won't be any point in Gwen not feeding from her. She'll be dying anyway."

"Ahhh, yes," Eilam cooed. "It would be a service to her. Do it."

Judging by the sick pleasure they were getting, I assumed that if she killed me first, it would still count toward her humanity.

I gasped as the shadow crawled on top of me. Zaro swung down, and the shadow's hand covered mine. We caught Zaro's hands, stopping the knife in midair. A coolness spread across my skin and into my bones, adding to my terror. The touch felt familiar. This whole thing was surreal, but this time, the shadow was saving me.

"What the—" Zaro's eyes widened. "How—"

I was surprised too. The shadow was *helping* me.

The shadow and I turned the tip of the dagger toward Zaro's chest. Sweat beaded on his lip as he struggled to regain control but couldn't.

"What's going on?" Eilam stood and stared at the scene before him. "How is that possible?"

"I ..." Zaro grunted, his jaw tense. "I... don't know."

Out of the corner of my eye, I watched as Gwen kicked Eilam's legs out from under him. He fell hard on his ass, and she blurred on top of him. Blood dripped from her nose onto his face.

"Annie, help!" Eilam demanded. "Like we discussed earlier."

My hands shook, but the shadow held them securely. The amorphous head nodded toward Zaro's chest. Creepy, but I understood what the thing was telling me. Together, we slammed the knife into Zaro's chest. It sank deep, like when I'd stabbed Darick. The vampire's mouth opened in shock, and he fell backward, the dagger protruding from his ribs.

"No!" Eilam screamed.

Eilam rolled on top of Gwen. Even though she was strong, she was much weaker than normal. He growled and punched her repeatedly, punishing her for what I'd done. The shadow helped me to my feet, even though I couldn't feel my legs. I stumbled toward them, but Eilam paid me no attention. His focus was purely on Gwen.

Barks erupted nearby, sounding like music to my ears. "She's in here!" Rosemary yelled.

Maybe I'd make it out of this after all. A loud *crack* sounded from above, and light spilled inside.

Veronica, we're almost there, Alex reassured me. *We're coming in.*

Something slammed into my side, and I fell away from the shadow. An arm tightened on my neck, and a knife cut into my skin.

My eyes flicked back to Zaro and the dagger still stuck in his chest. Annie must have had a blade of her own.

Her cold voice spoke right in my ear, "This is what you deserve, bitch."

After all of this, my life was going to end at the hands of my own sister.

The shadow raced toward me, not crawling anymore, desperate to save me as if it knew my death was imminent. My head grew woozy, and I realized that I might die before seeing my soulmate again. *Alex, I need you.*

A loud scream came from above as Alex's terror surged through me. The floor and walls shook all around. They were trying to get to me. All I needed to do was hold on, but the edges of my vision darkened.

ABOUT THE AUTHOR

Jen L. Grey is a *USA Today* Bestselling Author who writes Paranormal Romance, Urban Fantasy, and Fantasy genres.

Jen lives in Tennessee with her husband, two daughters, and two miniature Australian Shepherd. Before she began writing, she was an avid reader and enjoyed being involved in the indie community. Her love for books eventually led her to writing. For more information, please visit her website and sign up for her newsletter.

Check out my future projects and book signing events at my website.
www.jenlgrey.com

ALSO BY JEN L. GREY

Shadow City: Silver Wolf Trilogy

Broken Mate

Rising Darkness

Silver Moon

Shadow City: Royal Vampire Trilogy

Cursed Mate

Shadow Bitten

Demon Blood

Shadow City: Demon Wolf Trilogy

Ruined Mate

Shattered Curse

Fated Souls

The Hidden King Trilogy

Dragon Mate

Dragon Heir

Dragon Queen

The Wolf Born Trilogy

Hidden Mate

Blood Secrets

Awakened Magic

The Marked Wolf Trilogy

Moon Kissed

Chosen Wolf

Broken Curse

Wolf Moon Academy Trilogy

Shadow Mate

Blood Legacy

Rising Fate

The Royal Heir Trilogy

Wolves' Queen

Wolf Unleashed

Wolf's Claim

Bloodshed Academy Trilogy

Year One

Year Two

Year Three

The Half-Breed Prison Duology (Same World As Bloodshed Academy)

Hunted

Cursed

The Artifact Reaper Series

Reaper: The Beginning

Reaper of Earth

Reaper of Wings

Reaper of Flames

Reaper of Water

Stones of Amaria (Shared World)

Kingdom of Storms

Kingdom of Shadows

Kingdom of Ruins

Kingdom of Fire

The Pearson Prophecy

Dawning Ascent

Enlightened Ascent

Reigning Ascent

Stand Alones

Death's Angel

Rising Alpha